YOUNG BLOOD

SIFISO MZOBE

CATALYST PRESS
Vinton, Texas

In North America, this book is distributed by
Consortium Book Sales & Distribution, a division of Ingram.
Phone: 612/746-2600
cbsdinfo@ingramcontent.com
www.cbsd.com

Library of Congress Control Number: Forthcoming

Cover design by Karen Vermeulen, Cape Town, South Africa

This book is dedicated

to my township and yours

"The story pulsates with energy that makes it intense and very real. It is a voice that tells about crime and how it speaks to the youth through poverty...A thrilling, action-packed diamond in the rough."
Tshepo Tshabalala, *Tonight*

"This debut novel is a compelling journey through the underbelly of the streets of Umlazi Township, Durban, and marks the arrival of a fresh new voice on the South African literary scene."
Mbali Vilakazi, *Cape Times*

"With considerable panache, [Mzobe] lifts the lid on township life in Umlazi, focusing on the lives- and frequent violent deaths of the young bloods, the township high school dropouts who are faced with a stark choice. There is a good deal of raw power here, and an easy, fluent writing style. I hope we will hear more of Sifiso Mzobe."
Margaret von Klemperer, *The Witness*

"Young Blood is a sober account of the fate of many a young man. The question implied throughout is exactly how much young blood must be spilled before Siphore discovers his integrity."
Lara Sadler, *Cape Argus*

YOUNG BLOOD

Sifiso Mzobe

RIDING WITH
A RIDER

✸

I remember the year I turned seventeen as the year of stubborn seasons. Summer lasted well into autumn, and autumn annexed half of winter. It was hot in May and cold in November. The older folk in my township swore they had never seen anything like it. Winter nibbled on spring, and spring on summer.

It was exactly thirteen days to the day that I gave up on my high school education. There was absolutely nothing for me in school. My reports were collections of F's. I was a master mumbler in class. In mathematics I was far below average. Nothing in school made sense, and nothing had since grade one. By grade ten I knew it was not for me. A childish hope of some-day understanding had carried me through the lower grades. By May that year, that hope ran out of steam.

When I told my parents of my decision to drop out of school, my mother went into a rage that lasted two days. My father promised me a beating to end all beatings. I showed them my F's. After her anger had subsided, Ma listened to my explanations, but it was clear she did not understand. Nothing in class made sense, I told her. I was in grade ten, yes, but the last concepts I had really understood were at grade seven level, and I was average at those. In class, my mind was there for the first five minutes—five minutes in which I focused intently. But for the next thirty-five minutes my thoughts would wander, lost in a maze of tangents.

It was May, and the school soccer program had already been scrapped for the year because of a stabbing incident in the stands during an away game earlier in the year. The beautiful game was something I understood. I was a striker in the school team, and a gifted goal-getter. The soccer pitch was where I shone. It was going to be a long year, with me mumbling wrong answers in class and no soccer to redeem myself. The scrapping of the soccer program was not so much a reason I left school but rather a footnote.

We all slept on it. Over the next few days, the house was thick with tension. My parents enlisted the help of relatives. Uncles and aunts lectured me over the phone. School is important. Education is the key to a bright future. You are crazy, you should not have done what you did. I was polite, answered "yes" to everything, but my thoughts drifted away. I wished I had super-powers and could shove my school reports into the receiver to let them see the F, G and H grades that meant I did not have the key to a bright future.

My parents tried, they really did. Ma shouted, shook me, asked for more explanations; she tried to understand but could not—the same way I tried to understand in school but didn't. She even cried.

"I don't know what I will do, Ma, but I am not going to school. You see my reports; there is not one subject I pass. I can't do anything right in school. Every day I go there it's like a part of me dies. Ma, you see my reports every year, there is nothing for me there,"

I explained.

"But in this world, you don't just give up. You must keep trying," she said.

"I know, Ma."

My parents tried. My uncles and aunts tried. Days rolled on and their calls dried up. The tension in our house slowly lessened.

"At least he was honest with us about his decision. We know where he is. At least he is not like the others who pretend like they are going to school when they are not," I overheard Ma say to Dad.

❖

Thirteen days after I left school was my seventeenth birthday.

I was sitting on the wall that doubles as a fence and chilling area to our house, waiting for Musa, when I realized that all the trees on our street had shed their leaves. The wall, roughly painted sky blue on the outside but bare on top and inside, encloses the house in a crooked, incomplete circle. Back then, our four-roomed house wore a coat of plaster as a prelude to painting. This had taken me a day to sand down, which made my body ache in places where I did not know muscles to exist. It was not all in vain, though; at night, with all the streetlights out, the house gave off a dull glow—as beach sand sometimes does. It was close to midnight and I was thirsty.

Our house is meant to be the main feature of the ring on a cul-de-sac. Our blue wall takes up most of the space on the ring, which makes our house the last. The last on the road, the last to get plastered, the last to get a squeezing hug from the walls we call fences.

The plastering on our house had been done in pro-longed stages, starting with the walls in view—the front and one side. Construction of the wall took even longer. My father often fired builders, but to be fair to him most builders did not even bother to bring a spirit level. The work took years to complete, as something of greater importance always seemed to crop up—water and electricity bills, food, school uniforms and shoes.

A shopping mall had been built on the outskirts of the township, while the builders' sand grew grass and turned shrubby in our backyard. The paintwork on the wall was mine. It was a weird blue; I told Ma the paint had gone bad.

The process of purchasing the gate to complete the crooked circle of the blue wall was also pro-longed. My father had the idea of getting two dogs to guard the gap, but this went nowhere. We would feed the dogs during the day; at night, the gap was silent. Those strays disguised as pets were never there. Every week, Ma returned from the city with brochures and quotations for a gate. Months passed, and the money went on other things.

Our house, which is slightly slanted, sits at the end of 2524 Close in M Section of Umlazi. To this day perhaps, ours is the only road in the hills of Umlazi that is close to being flat. Mama Mkhize's Tavern stands at the entrance to 2524 Close. The gates to this oasis are forever open, the music always pumping. It is a refuge for all who prefer life lived nocturnally. I knew Musa would be late that evening, so I made my way there.

The moon was plump and yellow, like a sun just risen, and it gave 2524 Close a brilliant bluish shine in the darkness. The midday and afternoon bustle was as distant as yesterday's newspaper. As the night wore on, 2524 Close took on a crowded silence; the only signs of people passing were simple salutes and the minute amber circles of lighted cigarettes. A neighbor's daughter kissed a man in the back seat of a car. Around midnight, the smell of marijuana is everywhere in the township. I gulped down a cloud of smoke that crossed my path. The rhythm of my steps made the moon slide and dance a little.

Mama Mkhize sells beer in cans, quarts and by the crate, weed in plastic coin bags and Mandrax pills in singles and even packets. She is a dynamo of a woman, and there are rumors she is related to people for whom killing comes easily.

"My nephew, the one in Joburg, took his BMW to these things, what do you call them...agents? Six thousand rands, I tell you, just to have the engine fixed."

My two Amstels were in her right hand, four loose cigarettes and change in her left. She looked like she was about to give me a hug. Gold snaked around her neck in different layers, shining on her fingers and dancing on both wrists. Her arms were thin but muscular. I always felt things move inside me when I saw her; maybe it was the Diesel jeans she wore, which made her look like a teenager in full bloom. It was unfair that she had inherited the name of her business, for she was only in her late thirties, a fact I vehemently denied until I serviced her car and saw her driver's license. I had thought she was younger.

"Sipho, I can see you are still worried about last

week. Don't. You understood what I was telling you, so relax. I told you I understood, and it was just the liquor talking anyway."

To her list of attributes, I must add tact, for what happened "last week" was me crossing a boundary. It had been five days after I'd dropped the "school bomb" on my parents. The smoke from that explosion still lingered in my house, but I had woken up to a good day. I'd fitted brake pads to eighteen taxis at R50 per car. Bulging pockets drove sleep away that night. I felt ten feet tall, and bought a bottle of Johnnie Walker Black from Mama Mkhize.

It was a slow night, when even the twenty-four-hour taverns closed. Mama Mkhize clutched a bundle of keys as I poured my first triple. Courteous, she invited me into the house, and I was surprised by what transpired.

"Johnnie is my favorite too. Mind if I join? I'll give you a taste of my hand. I have Appletiser, soda water, tonic water and just water. What do you use?"

My choice of dash for the whiskey triple did not matter. The taste of her hand—light. Lots of soda water, a film of Appletiser. Easy on the senses.

"I could drink all night if I dashed like you. Light, but it goes down well," I said.

We drank and laughed. There was a cozy touch to the way we chilled. She made chicken livers as a snack. With each shot, her eyes slanted. She allowed me to get close. I was about to plant a kiss.

"Please leave," she said in a tone strong enough to knock sense into me. Yet I swear her eyes giggled through the whole thing. The following day, I was at her door with an apology that she accepted with no

YOUNG BLOOD

lecture attached. Since then, I had only stolen glances at her; eye-to-eye contact made me blush.

"Yes, the agents are expensive, but they have professionals and machines that measure the tiniest of details."

My attempt at bringing a natural, quick end to our conversation failed dismally.

"Nonsense, Sipho. He should have given the car to you. You know when you rev them, the windows of this house tremble."

Mama Mkhize was a natural exaggerator. Maybe she had to be. She dealt with drunks all day and sometimes all night. I took my beers, smokes and change. My eyes bowed to her direct stare. Her straight face with giggling eyes.

"Maybe next time he'll come to me. I will charge less than half of what he paid."

I headed home. I preferred solitude by the blue wall to solitude among drunks.

Musa's car was parked by the blue wall, doors ajar, when I got home. The colors—white on blue—had my mind retrieving a snapshot of summer skies over my granny's house at Amanzimtoti. The engine of the BMW 325is was humming. Beer in one hand, Musa was urinating into the concrete channel that drains 2524 Close.

❖

I knew Musa from the shantytown that occupied my backyard view. When I was seven years old, the shacks pasted on the hill mushroomed to form a functional neighborhood. A stream separated our M Section from them. When we were kids, our parents warned us about the shacks and the crooks who roamed there. I nodded my head but did not keep away because there was a shop there that had the sweetest, cheapest sherbets. They loved me at that tuck shop. The granny who owned it always pinched my cheeks and called me her son-in-law.

For every suburb there is a township, so for each section in the township a shantytown—add a ghetto to a ghetto. Fully functional, with such things as committees and such. The shantytown even had a name, Power, after the electricity plant that buzzed day and night at the top of the slope.

It was impossible not to mix with the children of Power because we shared a dusty patch by the stream that we used as a soccer pitch. I was eight years old when I first saw Musa, and I cheered in unison with the crowd for this boy who—though only ten years old—ran circles around the older boys. Musa was the king of football tricks. In twenty-cent games, he always put on a show. In my mind, when I think of our childhood soccer-playing days, I can't keep out this vision of a stickman running, the ball glued to his feet, dancing over tackles in a cloud of dust.

We also shared a school with the children from Power. In grade four I shared a desk with Musa, which is when he became my friend. I made the school's soccer team because of him.

On a football pitch, Musa passed the ball to death. What I lacked in showmanship, I compensated for with speed, blessed with pace and strong lungs. Everywhere on the pitch Musa's passes found me, through the eye of the needle, across a sea of legs. I would point to the spot and Musa would put it there.

In high school we were in separate classes, so we only hung together after school. When friends change, they get bored of chilling with you. Musa started to hang with the shoplifters—birds of the same feather, I reckoned. On days when he forced himself to pass by my house, our talk was no longer the same. I'd yap about engines and soccer while he rapped about the spoils of shoplifting—things to sell and money to collect.

Musa hung with the shoplifters, who in turn hung with the car thieves, all dressed up swank and bragging about which of the two cliques made cash quicker.

Although the signs had been there for a long time, it still came as a surprise when Musa dropped out of school in grade nine. He left for the City of Gold with only the clothes on his back. His return from Joburg— dressed fresh in Versace, in a car considered the holy grail of BMWs in the township—was drenched in a glorious "I have made it" glow.

❖

"You are a magician, Sipho. My car flies now. When I press it, it goes. I mean really goes. I hope you are ready because we are drinking tonight, birthday boy."

Musa's hands were in flight. He wore a brightly colored, shiny shirt.

His car really only needed a major service. He would have known this had he not just dropped the car and left. But Musa was never interested in that aspect of cars. He was present for almost all of my apprenticeship as a mechanic in our backyard, yet not once did he touch a spanner or change a brake pad.

He just sat on a piece of newspaper on our greasy bench and cracked up my father with his shoplifting tales.

"The secrets of these things are in the airflow meters. I played with it a little. Don't press it too hard or we'll have to rescue you from a bush somewhere. It is you who is the magician, Musa. Where did you get such a fresh 325is? It is beautiful, my brother," I said.

Musa rolled in a 325is that glided on seventeen-inch chromed BBS rims. Bar the rims, the car was original in all aspects, with all the electrical switches in proper working order. His 325is had the glassy shine of a Joburg car—as if there was a protective film over the paintwork. Even my father, a die-hard V8 disciple, was a fan of the 325is. A powerful engine on a light, balanced body. Graceful in the brutality of the drift. In the townships, the BMW 325is was—and still is—loved with the same passion by doctors and crooks alike. The sound in idle was a daring rumble.

"Put those in the back seat. There is a party waiting for us in Lamontville."

I threw my Amstels into the cooler box. A few sparks and then a flame revealed a devilish smile as Musa lit a cigarette.

"You drive, Sipho, I drank too much during the day. Start at Z Section—two girls we have to pick up there," he said.

We slid through to the brighter streets of Z Section, to the bigger new houses near my old primary school. As kids on the way home from school we were in wonder at the machines that sculpted the hill, accelerating the disappearance of the guava, mango, peach and mulberry trees that were once so abundant in

Umlazi. The new houses on the hill had yards the same size as our four rooms, as well as more bedrooms and an added lounge. These were the calmer parts of the township; the streets were quiet, and no adolescent cliques tried to break the night.

The 325is was flirtatious under my palms; the more I pushed it, the further it sat. Musa, my waiter, supplied cooler-box-cold beer. Under a yellow street-light, two shapes waved in silhouette. All I could make out were curves.

"Stop by the third light; it is them."

Musa hugged both girls and arranged the seating so that he was with the taller girl in the back seat.

"Please play me number six on this CD."

My companion in the front spoke with the ease of nightlife. A request from thick, heavily glossed lips revealed a full, warm smile. The flowery sweetness of perfume rushed up my nostrils when she moved closer to the stereo in search of the skip button.

"Below the volume knob," I said.

At stop streets, I stole looks at her. She turned up the volume and sang to the song. Gradually, I made out the contours of her face. Top-heavy oval, I confirmed under the fluorescent lights of a petrol station.

Township night-riding is strange, for there is an unspoken agreement which, although not binding, stipulates that we are instantly familiar. No need for formal introductions. I caught their names when they answered or made calls. We bought snacks at the petrol station shop. In the pay queue, Sindi, my companion in the front seat and the more curvaceous of the two girls, smiled and looked up at me. She offered one earphone of her cellphone radio.

"Listen. It's the same song we played in the car," she said.

In the reflection on the pay booth glass, I tried to check her out but found her already there. She forced a blush and smiled. We entered Lamontville through the back door.

A few streets from the venue I heard house music and followed it, my ears leading me to the exact spot. Our expectations were met by a convoy of cars. Musa jumped out of the 325is well before I turned off the ignition. The host was a friend of Musa's who went up and down the street and broke the night by spending a few minutes in each car. Whisky glass in hand, in each car he uttered the same words: "It's not even a party. I don't know who started this rumor. Could Durban be so boring that people have time for chitchat? We are all family, though. I mean, I was bored anyway and now I have booze to drink and chicks to look at. You are chilling on my street. I am giving you the freedom of the tarmac. Drift, spin, do whatever. Bang your system to the maximum if you like."

He passed out in Musa's car, quickly and suddenly, before the drifting started.

"It had to happen, Sipho. He drank from every whiskey bottle and smoked all the blunts busted near him," said Musa.

Loud whistles and laughter greeted Musa and me when we carried the host inside the house—a homely, tidily renovated four rooms with fully fitted kitchen, the tiles in the bathroom color-coded to the handwash basin and bathtub. He was a sucker for blue—the BMW under the carport, the bathroom, the curtains and the comforter in his bedroom. He was dead weight, a thud on the bed. Musa took off his shoes and rolled him to the center of the double bed. The blackout and the emptiness of the house were signs of his bachelor status. He was barely there when his eyes opened.

"Thanks, Musa. I'll call you tomorrow about that thing. Lock from the outside and throw the key here."

He pointed to the bedroom window. A loud snore sounded when we tossed the key inside.

The exercise provided much-needed fresh air, which was suddenly diluted by weed smoke as we moved toward our car at the end of the convoy. I knew some of the high rollers, most of whom were from my township. Musa knew everybody, though. He stopped at almost every car, and was saluted by their crews. I kept cool as the introductions nonchalant-ly rolled off. But I quickly headed for the car, bored with standing next to Musa while his friends eyed me up and down. And I needed to chase away the slight wave of sobriety that was creeping over me.

Our two companions were dancing by the 325is. The smell of petrol, coupled with the sound of high-revving engines, was heavy in the cool wind. It always starts with one car revving until the engine clocks. The shrieking of whistles meant it was time to use the freedom of the tarmac. In the township, they say the streets talk; a few handbrake turns will turn the streets to pages, with tires as black-inked pens.

The whistling climaxed as the first car started.

The roads in Lamontville are basically a touch wider than one lane divided into two. There was no space to drift really because of all the cars parked on one side of the road. The few pockets of space were at the apex of the convoy and at the base, one car behind us.

A red matchbox BMW 320i was the first to show off. It turned gently yet descended with fury, first gear pushed to the maximum and double taps on the accelerator when it shifted to second gear. Full throttle again to pass us as a red blur driven by smiling gold teeth. He pulled the handbrake, the wheels locked, and the 320i turned slightly over a half circle. It hardly stood still as whistles and screams filled the air. It ascended full blast but did not turn at the top.

"He is scared. It could have been better," I said, not meaning to voice my thoughts.

Sindi was next to me, our reflection in the windows of the 325is proclaiming us a seasoned couple.

"Maybe you don't even know how to do this, but you criticize," she said.

"It is nothing, I am telling you. I can turn it two, three, maybe four times where he did it once."

"Such a liar. You know, I have never been inside a spinning car."

"If you are not scared, you can ride with me. I will be the last to spin. We'll open the sunroof. You can wave to everybody."

A few more tried, but none were perfect turns. Our reflection was joined by another couple—Musa and his girl.

"Before you start, please take the cooler out, otherwise everything will spill all over my seats," Musa said.

"It's all right, Musa, there won't be a single drop."

"There is no way I am risking that."

"Key?"

"Are you really that drunk? The key is with you, Sipho."

Sindi's eyes were hesitant. I started the engine and gauged the handbrake and clutch, then tested it at full throttle while still. The 325is responded with a twitchy bounce. Through the sunroof I put out my hand and beckoned Sindi over.

"Come with a dumpy," I shouted over the engine.

She opened the door and sat down in one motion. I released the handbrake and stepped full power on the accelerator. The 325is stalled, and took a few digs on the tarmac. When I released the clutch, it was like we were inside a bullet. Sindi was pushed deep into her seat and let out a joyful scream. I went full on the gears, double-tapped the accelerator from first to second. Simply to show off, I tapped it three times from second gear to third. At the top of the convoy I changed it down to second, handbrake up. The 325is turned and stayed. Full throttle in neutral once again, all windows down. I heard whistles over the engine sound. I pushed it to metal to drown them out. When it clocked, I put it into first and second with double taps all the way down to the end of the convoy. The smell of burnt tires and weed smoke gushed in through the windows.

"When am I showing through the sunroof?" shouted Sindi.

"I'll tell you when we get down there," I said. Third, fourth, back to second and handbrake. The car turned a perfect one-eighty degrees.

"Now!" I said.

Sindi balanced her legs on both seats. She had ample space on both because, as I started to spin, the force of it all meant I was pressed against the leather of the door and used only half of my seat. I turned the 325is three full circles while she swayed through the sunroof. I peeked up: her face had the expression of a scream but I heard nothing over the engine. At the end of the last circle, I saw that the crowd had gathered around the 325is. I went full throttle in neutral. Every time the engine clocked Sindi banged her hands on the sides of the sunroof.

"Sindi, get down, I'm parking," I said.

"One more, please," she pleaded, with childish glee.

"Maybe later."

I parked on our spot. Cheers and whistles as we opened the doors. Sindi was out of breath.

"How was it, Sindi?"

Musa gave me high fives. Sindi had no words— just both thumbs up and an accusing smile directed my way.

The next car went full blast, only to hit the pavement on a turn. Both wheels on the impact side gave way, crumpling completely; the car nearly tipped over.

I was low-key for the remainder of the night. While Musa paraded his girl around, I was glued to the back seat with Sindi. She took off her jacket. My hand was frozen from the futile search for beer in the cooler box—only ciders remained.

"You guys can drink. Twenty-four beers just for the two of you?"

"You know it is cooler outside."

"I am comfortable here. Without the jacket I will cool down. You are scaring me—why are you looking at my mouth so much?"

"Your lips, Sindi."

"Do I have something on them?"

"No."

"What then?"

"They are beautiful. Like I can eat them or something."

She smiled and performed her shy-girl routine when I came closer.

"Wait! Let me wipe off this gloss first."

She retrieved a tissue from her handbag. A sequence of nibbling, tongue, nibbling and pause ensued.

"I am not going home. My mother is already on to us. She called the friend we said we were visiting. We might as well face her in the morning. I know Ma— she will be cooler then," Sindi said.

Smooches graduated to something more ferocious. The leather squeaked as she straddled me. Ebony women and their bottom-heavy shape seem to complement jeans. We nibbled on, breathing into each other beer, cider, cigarettes and the remnants of lip gloss—a faint strawberry flavor. Sindi removed my hands when I explored between her legs.

"Don't rush; we cannot do everything in the open like this," she said.

I cooled down, content with kisses because I was sure to score. Even if I had been blind, the signals did not come clearer than that. Deep in the groove of kissing technique exchange, we were disturbed by a knock on the back windscreen. It was a guy with gold teeth, the first one to spin in the red BMW.

"Sorry, bro, I thought you were Musa. Where is he, by the way?"

"Somewhere by the silver 7 Series up there," I said.

Sindi moved aside, rolled her eyes and tugged playfully at my T-shirt when I stepped out to attend to Gold Teeth.

Gold, gold and more gold. Hoops for both earrings, for each alternate tooth, a large chain around the neck and thick bracelets for both wrists. He was about my age and dressed in a Versace shirt. Trousers, belt with oversized buckle and shoes were all Hugo Boss. In his hand he clasped a clump of crushed weed.

"Do you have rolling paper?" he said.

"No, but maybe Musa does. He is coming this way; you can ask him."

Musa was jovial, hand in hand with his chick. When I looked at her, I saw the unnerving resemblance to Sindi as they sat next to each other in the back seat of the 325is.

"Vusi, where is my M3?" shouted Musa. A smile from Gold Teeth.

"You will get it, Musa. Do you have rolling paper?"

"I blame this weed. Rolling paper, rolling paper? It has been three months since I placed my order, Vusi. Just say if you can't get it and I'll place my order elsewhere."

"You won't believe this, Musa, but I have had three already. One even had a Rob Green conversion. But the thing with all of them is, they go dead within five minutes. And you know with these helicopters they have now, I have to split."

"Well, this money will not wait long for you. Get me what I want."

"For sure," Vusi said.

"Rolling paper is under the ashtray. Any beer left,

Sipho?"

"We are out," I said. "It's late, time for Johnnie anyway."

Vusi rolled a fat, cone-shaped blunt. When it was my turn to hit it, I turned to smiles and expectant eyes from the back seat.

"Do you want some?" I asked the girls.

Synchronized nodding of heads. I passed it on to both girls. Musa opened the Johnnie Walker Black. I remember taking the first sip, and Sindi snuggling next to me in the back seat. Then, from the top of the convoy, a black cloud in attack formation headed straight for us, smothering me.

❖

The first thing I saw when I opened my eyes was the blue wall. Then Musa on his phone. He puffed a cigarette and pissed into the concrete channel.

"I blame Vusi and his weed," Musa shouted over the phone. "Where is Sindi and your chick?"

"She is not my chick. Just some girls I met in town yesterday and bought them lunch. They both blacked out like you. I dropped them at N Section—cousin's house or something."

"That was strong weed, Musa."

I was struck by the faint blue of dawn when I stepped out of the car. The clock read 4:17.

"Is this the right time?" I said. "Yes."

"You kept your promise, Musa. You got me drunk on my birthday. Catch you later in the day."

"Sipho, wait. Here is the cash for fixing the car, although the way you were spinning it you may have to fix it again soon. All the crooks were asking about you."

"These cars were made for spinning, Musa."

"What will you do with the money, anyway?"

"I want to buy a phone."

"I got a spare phone. You can take it; then I'll only pay like a hundred rands or something."

"Musa, you are Mr. Money but always bargaining."

"This is a good deal I am giving you. Take a look behind the gear lever."

"I'll take it, thanks, Musa. Call you when I get a SIM card. Anti-hijack system."

"Go sleep, Sipho. You are mumbling now."

"No, Musa. Anti-hijacks. What makes M3s go dead within five minutes are the anti-hijack systems. Someone came to see my father with a similar problem. The anti-hijack in his car was going haywire, so we disconnected it."

Musa came close with a seriousness I did not know him to possess.

"Can you override them? Can you disconnect them?" he said. "Yes, I can do both," I said.

I pissed on the blue wall. In the mirror in my room, I saw myself drunk. On the small table by my bed I picked up the birthday card left by my girlfriend, Nana, sixteen hours earlier.

It read, "Happy Seventeen, Sipho, I luv you."

FLiRTiNG WiTH
THE GAME

I woke later that morning to my father's impatient knocks on my bedroom window. Before I'd gone to sleep, I left the window open just a peek as I never could stand the pungency of overnight alcohol breath, even my own. When my father tapped on the window, the aroma of his coffee slid through the gap and provided a welcome change of odor in the aftermath of a hard night's drinking. I recalled Nana's words, the ones I always heard whenever I tried to kiss her while drunk. The way she laughed at all my jokes yet squirmed when I came closer: "If your breath smells like this, imagine your insides, stomach and everything. I am definitely not kissing you."

"You have visitors. Why are you still sleeping so late?" Dad asked.

I heard him first as a distant echo that amplified to jolt me out of slumber.

I took a minute to scrutinize the room and confirm that all the landmarks were there—the stained ceiling, mirror, Nana's birthday card. I moved the curtain—made by Ma on her sewing machine before it died—and saw Dad under the bonnet of a mistiming Ford Courier. With him were two members of the Cold Hearts gang. I had seen the Cold Hearts at the party in

Lamontville, but they had never come to us before to have their cars fixed. My tongue was a mess of yeast, barley, weed, cigarettes, ethanol and chips, and my head felt heavy. Definitely bathroom first.

I knew about the Cold Hearts. They were blood-spilling brothers. They talked—when they did talk—as if emotion was painstakingly sucked out of each word, so much so that if you were to replace their original words with others, the sentences would still sound the same.

In the township, there were horror stories about the Cold Hearts. Their signature was on the cash-in-transit heist up at Stanger that left all the guards dead, as well as the bloody hijackings at Hillcrest, which had brought the flying squad into the township. The dis-emboweling of a taxi driver in broad daylight—over a parking spot—had township people shaking their heads in silent outrage. Was their insanity enshrined in brutality and sheer barbarism?

I had a question of my own: What did they want from me?

The older of the two Cold Hearts pulled me aside. He seemed okay, so we went outside, by the painted part of the blue wall. He was a short, stocky, bald-headed heap of pure muscle. Despite their reputation, the Cold Hearts neither drank nor smoked. I had not seen any of them talking to the girls at the party in Lamontville. In the boisterous party atmosphere, they were blank-faced and aloof, and sipped only soft drinks.

He looked up at me with eyes so blank I wondered if anything functioned behind them.

"Help me with this. I hijacked a car and drove it all

the way from Hillcrest. I even went to the party in it. Now when I want to take it to the buyer it won't start. I hear you are good with these things. Can you start it for me?"

It did not sound like a question, so I did not answer. Only when I saw a slight crease on his forehead did I inquire, "How much will you pay me?"

"Don't worry, we will pay you," he said.

"I just need to know. I like everything out in the open. I have had people come here just like you, but in the end I don't get paid."

"Don't worry, you will get paid," he said.

"If your problem is what I think it is, I will charge you R800."

"We will pay you," he said again.

"Let me get my things, then. How far away is this car of yours?"

"First line of houses behind the church in G Section."

In the fog of a hangover, I collected wires and pliers from our toolbox by my father's legs.

"Do they have a problem with wiring?"

"The way they describe it, I think so, Dad."

"Before you go, can you start this car?"

The ignition on the Ford Courier only turned. There was no spark.

"Okay, stop. Will you pass any shops on your way? I need the paper, and bread for when your sister comes back from school."

"I'll see, Dad."

"Those are expensive pliers, please come back with them. You keep losing tools but you never replace them."

"I will, Dad."

When I saw the car supposed to take us to G Section, I felt a sickening ball of fear which I first dismissed as heartburn. It was the latest BMW 3 Series—not even the yuppies and taxi owners had it yet. I had felt such fear only once before—a year before, almost to the day, when I'd crashed a car into a concrete barrier on my sixteenth birthday.

Everything stopped. My heart and lungs took time out. I felt severe nausea when I closed the door and sank into the cream leather seats. It became almost unbearable when I saw that the upholstery around the ignition had been torn out and a screwdriver used to start the engine. The icy storm of the air conditioner, and the absence of a license disc on the windscreen, sent a single stream of cold sweat down my back. The reservations I had about starting a hijacked car in G Section were zero compared to R800. I would work fast, get the job done, take my cash and disappear in fifteen minutes. But the car supposed to take me to G Section was also stolen. This added an unforeseen, worrying dimension to the matter. The ride to G Section in a stolen car was not part of the calculation.

The Cold Hearts went wild with the car's gadgets, like children let loose in a toy shop. Thick fingers poked the sunroof button, while the taller and younger one set the air conditioner to full blast. I needed fresh air, but thought of fingerprints being dusted off the window button and quickly cancelled that idea. The younger Cold Heart turned to me in the back seat, a dead gaze on his boyish face.

"What is your problem? Why are your eyes bulging

YOUNG BLOOD

out?" I pointed to the windscreen.

While they were playing with all the gizmos inside the car, Musa had parked right in front of us, blocking the way. He got out, his face a mask of revulsion. He spat on the tarmac and called over the older Cold Heart. They crouched in the space between the two cars. Musa did not answer my greeting, and he just stared at the gangster. The ball of fear in my throat dissolved when he spoke.

"You are trespassing, brother. This here is my soldier. There must be a very good reason he is in your car. You better be giving him a lift or something."

Musa had his thumb in front of his face. When 26 gang members crouch to resolve issues, the raised right thumb is the sixth digit, on the presumption that all fingers of the left hand have been counted. Musa had his thumb up. The sign of the 26 gang. That six briefly turned into a seven when he pointed at me.

"Nice party at Lamontville yesterday," replied the Cold Heart. "And I must say it was nice when you played your cars, though personally I find it to be plain showing off. But girls like it. We are brothers, you and I, money lover. The very thumb you raise up, I was raised on it. My body is a gallery of medals. We can go there from dusk till dawn, Musa. You have never seen your kind wild like me, two and six."

The older Cold Heart rolled up both sleeves of his shirt.

"You see, Mr. Superstar from nowhere, everything written on this body tells a story. I am a captain, I have led teams and pushed schemes in and out of prison. Do not fluke me because I know this: the law of the number says it does not matter if it is my soldier or your soldier as long as we get money. Or has the law of the number changed? I hear in Westville Prison you can buy the number these days. Did you buy it, Mr. Superstar? Who are you, to speak of soldiers? What do you know about the thumb you raise to my face?"

"It is all the same, money lover. It is still as I say: my soldier is coming with me. We have money to make," Musa said.

"Money lover, we were also on a mission that was smooth sailing until you came along. Who do you think you are? Do you know you can die for this?"

"Man from the east, money over everything. A captain never talks to a general like this. I am a general here; in essence, I run things."

Musa took off his T-shirt. The tattoo over his heart showed two playing cards: a two of spades and a six of flies. Its appearance averted the threat of violence, for the younger Cold Heart had climbed out of the car with a knife in his hand. He silently moved away.

"It is as I said—my soldier is coming with me." Musa crouched firm.

Tattoos in prison are like certificates in society or medals in the army. The Cold Hearts were ready to take out Musa, yet the law of the number proclaimed him untouchable. The older Cold Heart stood up and retreated with a shake of the head. Musa parked the 325is on the side of the road. I realized, as the Cold Hearts sped off, that the ball of fear had vanished— and that my father's pliers were gone.

I am a township child; I knew what Musa and the Cold Heart were on about. I knew that what I had just witnessed was the law of the number of convicts, as laid out only briefly in number lore. I knew what the stars tattooed on my father's shoulders stood for. I knew that the stars were emblems from his past life as a lieutenant in the 26 prison gang. I knew that the 26 gang was for the money. When I was about twelve, I asked my father about his stars. Dad looked at me with regretful eyes, shook his head, and said, "It is just a fairy tale, son. My boy, never believe in fairy tales."

I also knew that the tattoo Musa showed to the Cold Heart indicated a high rank in the 26s. It was neither pretty nor clean, but rugged jail art. I knew at that moment that, during his time in Johannesburg, Musa had spent time in jail, and, as an all-rounder, had excelled in that side of life too—so much so that he was badged a general. The Cold Hearts were gone, but Musa was still scowling.

It dawned on me, as I looked at him, that Musa's life had unraveled in a peculiar manner.

❖

Musa was born in Nongoma, true dustlands where the tropical flavor of coastal KwaZulu-Natal is just a figment of the imagination. He arrived in Power, aged ten, to stay with his aunt who was not really his aunt because there was a break in the bloodline when their family tree was properly traced. Musa lost both his parents to tuberculosis the year he turned ten. The lady who took Musa in was a childhood friend of his mother. When Musa arrived in Power, his aunt was also close to my mother because they attended the same church. This was way back when the religious bug was still strong in Ma. Musa's aunt also helped out with household chores while Ma was recovering from giving birth to my sister, Nu.

Musa arrived in Power to a crowded shack, for his aunt had children of her own, as well as other children who were distant or imaginary relatives sent to her—just like Musa.

Musa was different from the other children of Power. On the dusty patch we used as a soccer pitch, the other boys ran bare-chested. They wore only shorts, citing the heat as the reason for their dress code. But we all knew they could not afford T-shirts. Musa always wore T-shirts. In twenty-cent soccer games, Musa never lost. He was different.

The teachers in school loved Musa because he was blessed with an absorbent brain. It was as if he were in class to prove false the concept that says repetition is the father of learning. Musa heard it once and never forgot. On weekends, he was never short of gardening offers from our teachers. Most of us begged to clean their gardens and yards for pocket money, but the teachers always chose Musa. When Saturday lunchtime matches began at the dusty pitch, Musa always had money in his pocket.

Life was hard at his aunt's shack. Sometimes, when I woke up too early for school and just sat in our backyard, I saw all the children who lived at his aunt's shack leaving for school and wondered how all of them managed to sleep in such a small space. With the proceeds from his gardening gigs, Musa bought what a child should not have to buy for himself—food and clothes. There was something too mature about him. I never saw a child take care of himself like Musa did.

Unlike me, he was an all-rounder. I was a good soccer player but a dismal student. Musa did everything well—school, soccer, he even did athletics for our school. He was good at everything, and when the shoplifting bug infected the township Musa caught the most acute strain. He excelled at shoplifting too.

When Musa dropped out of high school, three teachers crossed the stream to his aunt's shack. I was in the backyard at home and saw them talk to Musa for over an hour. A few days later, he passed by my house with a hurried step.

"I am going to Joburg. I hear things are better there," he said.

"When?" I inquired.

"Now," he said.

For a year and six months, that was the last I'd heard of him. The crouching duel in number lore with the Cold Heart had taken place on only his second week back from Johannesburg.

❖

"Drive me to F Section, I have to see a friend there." The look of revulsion was still on Musa's face.

He neither spoke nor flirted with girls at bus stops and on the pavement. He just smoked, with a scowl so vicious I did not dare ask for a puff.

"It was just something to direct, Musa, R800 for hardly fifteen minutes," I said, keeping my eyes on the road.

Apparently, there was something very wrong with my attempt to break the ice.

"Do not tell me about things to direct. All of a sudden you know the Cold Hearts. My friend, peel your eyes because you are rolling with me. Or should I peel them for you?"

His tirade continued when I shook my head.

"I think I should. One—you are with the Cold Hearts—by association you are guilty. In a stolen car with no license disc, no number plate. What were you thinking, Sipho? They call themselves 26 but spill blood like 27s. Their code is kill for whatever. Do you know what happens when you are arrested in a situation like this? The police beat you up before they hear your story. They won't care that you had nothing to do with the stealing of the car you are in. They put you in this thing called a tube and suffocate you. After that, all you can muster is a confession. Then comes the hard part—the bail money, the lawyer fees. A lousy R800 you were never going to get anyway is not worth all this trouble, because the Cold Hearts don't pay. Country crooks who came to the city for money; the only thing they know is how to take.

"I don't want you riding with these snakes, Sipho. Because they saw you spinning yesterday, they will approach you looking for a getaway driver. If anyone comes to you with that shit, tell them to come see me. None of them will pay you. I will put you on in a scheme for money if you are fearless. Remuneration for bravery must make sense. Fuck their schemes. I will put you on a sweet scheme."

By the time we reached F Section, Musa had cooled off a bit. "Stop by the third house on your right. Vusi lives here," he said.

The crooks who lived in F Section called it France for no other reason than the letter "F." The streets bustled like most sections of the township, but F Section did so with greater hustle. Three boys who were hardly thirteen years old stood opposite where we parked.

"Ask him," I heard them whisper as we closed the doors of the 325is. Musa turned to them.

"What do you say, nephews? What do you have for me today?" he said.

"A stereo, bra Musa, one of the latest ones with a face that flips."

"I'm never buying from you again. The stereo you sold me last week does not work. How much for this new one you are talking about?"

"R300," they answered simultaneously.

"Your price is too high. If you can work out a better price, maybe I'll buy it when I finish here."

"But, bra Musa, we are three—a hundred for each."

"Go collect it so I can see it, and maybe we can work something out."

The boys ran off.

"I am at the back!" Vusi shouted from the backyard as Musa was about to knock on the front door.

Vusi sat on a stripped-out car seat, both feet resting on an empty beer crate. A dumpy sweated on the ground next to him.

"You have good timing, brothers. I have just returned from town, hardly thirty minutes ago. How are you?" Vusi said.

"All right. Where were you?" said Musa.

"At the chest clinic in the city. My uncle, Sazi, had an appointment."

"How is he? The last time I saw him, he was really sick."

"Considering then and now, I will say better, but he is still sick. Most of the time he is in bed, like now."

Vusi offered beer, but we both declined. I accepted his cigarette, though—and the deal he put on the table.

"It is good you are here because I will need your help. I have to finish stripping this car by two in the afternoon. If it was not for Sazi's appointment, I would have finished a long time ago," Vusi said. In the shade of a makeshift carport, a top-of-the-range Nissan Sentra stood on bricks.

"You can steal cars for other people, Vusi, but I have to beg you for my M3. I placed my order with you when I was in Joburg. What did you do with the mag rims of this car, anyway? I know someone who has wanted them for months."

"You should have told me. I gave them to someone who has not paid me yet. So will you help me or what? The buyer has called me three times already confirming the time."

"How much will my cut be?" Musa said.

"The guy will buy everything for R8000. I'll give you R3000. You can put in the quiet king of drifting and cut half with him. I am serious, Musa, this is an emergency job. We should be on it as we speak."

Musa looked at me with an inquiring smile.

"What do you say, Sipho? Are you down for R1 500?" I just nodded my head.

"Good then, Musa. You will be on the doors, bonnet and boot. Sipho, you will be inside, and I can take the engine apart."

"No ways," Musa said. "I have money to collect and people to see. I'll check you grease monkeys after two."

It was just after eleven when we started. From his room in the backyard, Vusi salvaged a toolbox my father would have died for, an angle grinder and a six-pack of beer.

"Is beer all right? I have water and cold drink if not." I settled for water.

"You have to be neat, now. The buyer owns a scrap-yard so he is looking to resell the parts."

Vusi handed me a set of screwdrivers and small spanners.

He changed into overalls, the top half rolled and tied at his waist, but the gold remained. I took off my T-shirt and sat down on a beer crate for balance inside the car. The front seats were already stripped out.

Vusi was short and thin. Tiny in a way that made it a certainty that not much about his frame would change in the future. Musa and I looked young, but with elongated frames. Vusi looked fourteen. What he lacked in stature he made up for in boundless energy. Vusi looked young, yet his words were driven by a force twice his real age. There was a smooth way to his demeanor that strongly hinted at criminal experience. His shoulders were strong and muscled in a weird way, too defined for the rest of his body, like they developed too soon, and the rest was still catching up. He went through the task with a relaxed face, but worked fast, with controlled energy, like a person doing what they know they are good at.

Through the gap of the open bonnet I saw that it was not trial and error with Vusi. He knew the correct spanner sizes for the engine parts. When he reached for his tools, his hand returned with the exact-sized spanner. His shoulders locked, muscles strained, bolts and nuts popped and his tiny hands swiveled them out. Vusi took the engine apart methodically. He was mechanical in the task, clear about what came out first, like he had done it a thousand times before. Neat too, with all the nuts in one pile. Consumed by the task at hand, he did not say a word as he worked. I concentrated on my part of the job inside the cabin and mimicked Vusi's mechanical ways.

In thirty minutes, the inside of the cabin was finished, and just the pedals and wires remained. I joined Vusi on the outside. Ten minutes for the front and back lights, as well as the grille. We took a five-minute smoke break and cooled our faces with tap water.

"Will you smoke if I roll a blunt?" Vusi was busy crushing weed.

"Sure. I want to smoke it sober today. Yesterday your weed killed my night with the darkest blackout I ever had."

"After you finished spinning, nothing happened anyway. Those cowboy country nuts—the Cold Hearts—started fights and shot guns in the air. All the girls were scared. You can spin a car, Sipho. All the crooks were asking about you."

"I was raised around cars. My father is a mechanic, and you know how some people leave their scraps and never return for them. I helped my father fix the scraps, and in return he let me drive around in them. When he was away, I practiced spins in them. But the 325is, Vusi, that machine was made for spinning."

We revved the blunt. I downed it with water. Vusi guzzled beer. I looked at the Nissan Sentra—the victim of our destruction. It smiled a toothless grin.

The midday sun chased away the morning breeze, so we worked faster.

"Better we sweat once and finish. It will be hotter soon. We are almost done anyway. It is just the shell we have to cut in half, and the engine block, but the block I am not selling. I'll take it to the recycling people at Isipingo. There they pay by weight. I must get a quotation from your father, Sipho. There is a chisel-shaped RSI he needs to look at for me," Vusi shouted through the sound and sparks of the angle grinder.

"What is wrong with it?" I shouted back.

"It mixed water and oil, so the engine has no power. It has been parked for two months now. How much do you think he will charge me?"

"He'll take the cylinder head to the engineers to skim or do whatever is needed. Then put it back again. The engineers' fee will determine the price."

"And like that we are finished. You can wash your face and hands in the bathroom inside the house. Do it quietly because my uncle is asleep."

I heard the horn of the 325is through the bathroom window over the beeps and rumble of a reversing truck. A violent cough from a room opposite the bathroom echoed through the house. Two men were loading the broken Sentra, like pieces of a jigsaw puzzle, onto the back of the truck.

"Here is your money, Sipho. Thank you, my brother. You really helped me out. Musa is waiting for you outside."

"I am the one who should be thanking you, Vusi," I said.

"We will organize about the RSI."

"No problem. Come see me when you are ready,

Musa knows the way to my house."

I left Vusi arguing with the driver of the truck about the engine block.

"How much did he give you?" Musa said. "I did not count it."

"Count it before we leave."

"It is R3000 exactly. Here is your share."

I placed fifteen R100 notes in Musa's palm. He returned five of them.

"Thank you for this, Musa," I said. "No need, Sipho, you worked for it."

"Can we go to the city? My girlfriend is at the movies with her friends at Musgrave Center. I must also buy a SIM card for my phone."

"Is she pretty? I made a resolution this year: only pretty girls ride in my car."

"You'll see," I said.

THE PLAN

We arrived at Musgrave Center to the end-of-the-day buzz of shopping malls. Elongated afternoon shadows rushed to the bus stop, some to taxis, a few to their cars, while others stuck together in the various steady walks of love. I parked the 325is behind the metered taxis opposite the bus stop. Musa turned his head faster than a meerkat as girls passed by. He was like a glutton at a buffet, uncertain about which pavement to choose—our side of the road, where girls in two-piece suits headed for the parking lot to their cars, or the bus stop, where mostly students waited for public transport. His gaze fastened on the bus-stop side. "Check out the dark-skinned one holding oranges in that clique of fair skins," he said.

"I told you you'll see. That's her. That is Nana, my girlfriend."

"That is a girlfriend and a half, Sipho!"

I knew Musa did not believe me, but Nana acted it out for him. Her clique became instantly irrelevant as soon as she saw my waving hand. I loved the way she walked, as if stepping on sand. I did not understand yet somehow grasped that she loved me, even though she lived in a mansion at leafy High Ridge in N Section, which was practically a suburb within the township. My father's house looked like the servants' quarters at her house. Her father was a lawyer. Her dark complexion, dimples and large whiter-than-snow-on-TV eyes came from her housewife mother.

"Hi baby, did you enjoy the rest of your day yesterday? I waited for your call until I fell asleep. How are you?"

Her hug was warm, the peck she allowed me polite, for she was not a fan of public kissing.

"I am all right. Ma hid the telephone key again so I could not call. What's with the oranges, baby?"

"Ma said I must give them to your mother."

She waved to her friends, who were all giggles. Musa slid into the back seat.

"This is my friend, Musa, by the way."

"Hi, Musa, nice to meet you."

"Hi, Nana. Thank you for helping my friend; I am happy he has someone. Sipho, can we pop into Westville for a few minutes? I have an appointment at four."

I have this stupid notion of rating people by how good they look in cars. Nana got a perfect score for the 325is. She made it look whiter. Her dimples were at their best in a half smile—like right there and then.

"Baby, you know I have to be at home by six o'clock," Nana said.

"We won't be long," I convinced her.

We stopped to fill up the tank at a garage on Berea Road. I sent Nana to buy soft drinks, cigarettes and a starter pack. Musa strolled around on a call. The petrol attendants asked to look at the engine. They were joined by two white men in their forties and a formally dressed black guy. Just for show, I started the engine and pressed the accelerator for one hard rev. Nana returned and stood by my side. Then a black BMW M5—circa 1988, and spotlessly clean—entered through the exit of the petrol station and stole everyone's attention. Musa ran to the M5. He was in conversation with the driver for barely a minute, but when he came to us there was something different about his face, the lightness of a smile that ran from ear to ear.

The 325is displayed its rage on the N2. I could not resist—in places, that freeway has four fat lanes. I was lucky the speedometer did not work, because Nana was always alert in a car, glancing at the speedometer several times a minute. I was probably doing 180 km/h, yet there were no remarks from her or seat belt warnings. She was uncharacteristically calm and not even wearing her seat belt. While she applied lip gloss, she told me about the movie she had seen. She did not feel the speed. If it rides on four wheels, the suspension must definitely be sporty.

I did not know the way to Musa's house, so I reduced speed when we entered the suburbs of Westville. I recalled some of the streets we powered through. A friend of mine once took me to a party in the same area. On that weekend, my uncle Stan from Pietermaritzburg was down for a visit. Uncle Stan rolled in a big black BMW 735i. He gave it to me for the whole weekend. I still meet girls who were at that party; they think I'm rich. Being no mood killer, I go with the flow.

The air you breathe changes in the suburbs. There are more trees than houses, more space than you can imagine. The silence is healthy, the peace of mind a priceless asset. It is the kind of place you should be in if you want to be the fastest forward.

Musa lived at the end of a street whose name I never saw—the sign was hidden behind trees. It was the most peaceful place I have ever visited. His house was a contained, face-brick cluster. Space seemed absent upon entry, but the backyard was where the land was. The gradual slope felt like a park—there were even park benches. The balcony looked out onto houses scattered amid the trees. Space is what I see when I think of that house. In the lounge there were black leather sofas big enough to sleep on comfortably. The lounge looked out onto the balcony.

Nana turned on the TV. The program was music videos. She watched intently. We smoked weed on the balcony.

"Do you know the driver of the M5 I was talking to at the garage?" Musa said.

"Not really, as in riding and rolling with him, but I have seen him around. He's very down low, though he disappears for long periods to return with a faster car. Isn't he friends with the owner of the garage in R Section? I have seen his car there," I said.

"You are right. He used to scheme with those people. He made me a proposition, but I want you and Vusi to be in on it as well. He is a quick, smooth mover. You won't regret this, Sipho. Do you remember the remuneration talk we had this morning? This is that type of thing. He put me on some fast money up in Joburg. His name is Sibani—the purest of all money lovers. He is a quick thinker, but most important of all he is fair."

I watched Musa as he talked—his eyes turning

crimson by the smoke from the blunt. His matter-of-fact speech and serious expression were today's story to yesterday's journey of carelessness.

"We have to see Vusi first and I'll lay it out for you. Damn! I don't have any food in the house. What do you want to eat?"

"Nana, what do you want to eat?" I shouted.

Nana turned down the volume and came to the balcony. "Anything," she answered softly, as if turning down my own volume. We eventually decided on Nando's chicken. While Musa was out getting the chicken, I snuggled next to her on the sofa. She smiled and gave me peppermints to counter the smell of ganja. I perceived this to be a sign that read deep kissing ahead.

My favorite part of Nana's body is the curve at the back of her waist. I touched her ear, and felt her heat. Lips locked, we rotated in slow motion. I slid my hands down, felt the contours of her hips. Seeing all was in rhythm, I touched the top of her thigh. Lecture time.

"Baby, we can only kiss."

"But why, Nana? You know I love you."

"I love you too, baby, but I am not ready yet."

"Can you give me a time, then? An estimation of when? Baby, it has been a year. How many more months until you are ready?"

"Don't get like that, baby. We will do it when I am ready."

I had never had intercourse with Nana. Physical love would solidify what we had. I stated this. Instead, she gave me lectures on readiness. I didn't understand —and still don't—how anyone could make tall tales from so meaningless a word. I went to the balcony, smoked a cigarette and a blunt in succession to let my erection subside, and gave her zero for conversation.

All the women in my life say I handle rejection like a spoiled child. I hear them, but I won't change. If you don't want to do what I want you to do, for that minute or hour or day, we have nothing in common. We might as well not relate.

Musa returned with the food. He joined me on the balcony while Nana set the chicken on plates.

"When I left you were all smiles. What's the problem now? Is there trouble in Loveland?" he mocked.

"She is playing with me, my brother. We have been going out for a year of no sex."

"I feel for you, Sipho, but flip this coin. Look at it this way: Your problem is rare. Girls with brains want it to mean something. You can see that, at least."

Our meal—chicken and chips with Coke—went down in silence. Nana slowly took bites of her chicken. She mimicked a frown, her lips pursed. In all honesty it made me laugh, for she looked like a little girl. Musa answered the intercom through a mouthful. He hurried for a change of shoes.

"My appointment is here. Here is the key—make sure you lock up when you go. Take my car. I will call and we can meet up in the city later. Bye, Nana, I hope we can meet again in a more festive atmosphere," he said.

I ate in silence. Nana picked sulkily at her chicken. We sat on separate sofas, indifferent to each other. I tried to activate my starter pack but the battery on my phone was dead. Stretching out, I flipped through the channels. She washed the plates and glasses.

"When will we leave, baby? I don't want to be late."

"We can go now, even." I grabbed the keys from the table.

On the freeway, I nearly clocked the 325is, stopped short by Nana's sobs. I did not look at her directly during the trip to her house. Out of the corner of my eye, I could see she had a tissue over her face.

"I don't know what you are crying for, Nana. I am the one who is not loved here."

She let out a torrent, which eased when we entered the township. I dropped her off with no goodbye kisses.

❖

"Mus-sa called. He s-said you s-should meet him by the 320 at s-seven o'clock."

My little sister Nu was watching cartoons when I got home. She was ten years old, and still sucked her thumb. My best friend since birth, she even talked with the thumb in her mouth—a habit that deeply irritated Ma. The family had learned to understand her, even with the added s's in her speech. As for the neighbors, their conversations with Nu were kept to a minimum. It was close to six o'clock. Ma was getting ready for work.

My mother worked as a cleaning lady at Clairwood Hospital near Lamontville. She sometimes worked night shifts, and there was no warmth at home when she was gone. She had the gift of making meager resources suffice. There were times in my childhood when I did not know exactly what her occupation was. Before her sewing machine gave out, she sewed clothes. There was also a period when she sold Tupperware. Now she made extra cash selling home-made pies.

"I have been waiting for your father. He went to test the Ford Courier an hour ago, but he still has not returned. He'll make me late for work."

Ma sat next to Nu on the sofa, her handbag and steamy, transparent pie container placed neatly on the coffee table.

"What time does your shift start?"

"Half past six. Are you driving? Please take me if you can. My boss is strict about punctuality."

"After I shower, Ma," I said.

I gave Nu the leftover Nando's. She replaced her thumb with chicken.

The shower was bad timing, for the hot tap sprayed me with cold water. The geyser must have been switched off to save electricity. I was in and out faster than in a robbery. I thought of Nana while I got dressed and wondered whether she really loved me.

"Hurry up, Sipho, or I will be late," Ma shouted.

She organized Zodwa, our neighbor's daughter, to babysit Nu. "Who are you fixing this car for?"

"Musa."

"There must be money in Joburg. What has it been —a year or so? And he has bought himself such a beautiful car. Where is he working?"

"He only returned the other day, Ma. I have not had time to ask him about that."

"Your aunt Bessie called. She wants you and Nu to go up to Bloemfontein for the holidays."

We were at the last robots out of the township;

streams of cars were entering and departing. Return dayshifters, exit the nightshifters.

"It is cold up there, Ma."

"Well, Sipho, you must call her and say so, because she will be expecting you."

Aunt Bessie lived well. She had a butchery and supermarket in her own shopping complex. She had married some politician guy she met at varsity. Aunt Bessie gave us cash just to visit her. I was fine with the money part; the drawback was boredom and the chills of a Free State winter. Her children—my cousins —spoke English all the time, with a snobbish accent. I was down with none of that plastic life.

"Take a pie. I made spinach for supper and I know you don't like it."

"Thanks, Ma."

I dropped her off at the main gate of Clairwood Hospital.

For a car that breathes as freely as a BMW 325is, Durban's West Street is best at night. It is empty, so the robots are there to be raced. The sky is pitch black, the streetlights a bright orange. The sound from the tailpipe reverberates off the buildings as if the high-rises, banks and chain stores have their own engines. I hit West Street a few minutes before seven. The 320 Building is where the city stands.

At night, there are suburban and township girls in equal numbers. The upper classes wait for daddy's car to take them home; the hardcores for anything out of the city.

Musa was finished with business by the time I arrived at the 320. We tried to sweet-talk some girls, who would not give us the time of day. Locating Vusi was not a problem—everyone in the city knew him. We found him by the inconspicuous beaches beyond Willows and the Durban Country Club.

He was there with a crew of eight—five girls, three boys. His gestures and posture screamed township. They were sitting under a gazebo, highly weeded. A braai was in full flight, and there were two cooler boxes packed with liquor.

"Brothers, to what do I owe the pleasure? I guess I can never hide in this Durban," said Vusi, flashing his gold grille.

"We need to talk," said Musa.

He did not have to add anything to entice Vusi into the 325is. The radio was switched off.

"I know both of you are serious about money. Well, here is a chance to make it. My friend...no, my brother, Sibani, told me about a hustle he has for me and two other people. What we'll do is steal cars—real cars, six cylinders and above—change the tags, engine numbers and color, and sell them. We'll take them across borders if we have to. Sibani and I will raise the cash for paperwork and extras. All you two must do is get the cars."

I had recently helped my father disconnect a troublesome anti-hijack system. Musa knew this. I had never stolen a car. Musa knew this too.

"I hear, Musa. I understand you, my brother. The problem is, I have never stolen a car before," I said.

"It is not the hardest thing in the world, Sipho. Otherwise there would not be so many car thieves in the townships. The actual stealing is not complicated.

Finding the heart to go steal is the hard part. You have to want to do it; that is the only way you will learn. Vusi, you are all quiet; what do you say?"

"I have been under a gang before, Musa. You know it is the runners that get less, even though they are the fire."

"You have not heard the best part yet. When you bring us a car, we will pay you a few thousands—cash just to move around—but when we sell these cars, at just below the market value, half is for you two, the other half is for us."

"Don't be so quiet, Sipho. Say something," Vusi said.

"I am thinking we should not ride these cars much. Digital odometers are hard to turn back, and mileage is what buyers look at most in cars," I said.

"In fact, we will drive them only when taking them to the buyers. Must I take this nodding of heads as a yes?"

Vusi and I nodded again.

"Sibani will give us the list in a few days. Business is over. Who are those chicks, Vusi?"

"Some suburban chicks we picked up at the 320. There are some fly ones, though. You see the one..."

That was how it went down. I heard it as I listened to the ocean. I did not even try to go against the tide. One girl rode me on the sand, so slow it seemed to never end. We smoked weed until sunrise.

YOUNG MAN, IT STARTS HERE

◆□◆□◆□◆

Almost all the people I called my peers were second-generation township dwellers. When my father said he was going home, he embarked on an exhausting, bumpy drive to the rural south coast, past Umzumbe and beyond, to dusty villages where youths still greeted elders. I went there too from time to time. There was nothing lavish about the place. When I said I was going home, I meant Umlazi—a township. Both my maternal and paternal grandparents were of the last generation that lived in the same place for their whole lives. Times changed fast. Even I, bush mechanic that I was, vowed not to die in a township, let alone in my father's house. My father had been a hustler in his past life. Brave and wild. He may not have shown it, but I knew he was proud when he saw me make money. Even in our backyard, Dad always passed customers on to me and let me keep the money. That morning, he was focused on fine-tuning an engine. The hum of the Ford Courier may have sounded perfect to other ears, but with Dad it was paramount that every car pass the coffee-cup test before he proclaimed his work done. Ma told me he used to drink and smoke back in the day, but when I was born coffee replaced liquor and cigarettes. My father drank a minimum of ten cups of coffee a day. Through the spring, summer, autumn and winter, he sipped hot coffee from his giant, ageless enamel cup.

It was the same cup he used for his test. If the job was engine-related, Dad filled the cup with water and placed it over the cylinder-head cover of the tuned engine. If the vibrations did not spill the water over the rim of the cup, the job was proclaimed perfect. A spill meant he started all over again.

I related with my father on a comfortable, balanced level. Casual, but with respect. He treated me as if I used my brain. For that alone I would always defend him. When his friends came to get their cars fixed and he was not there, they told me stories about his past. The theme was always bravery and speed. I knew I had inherited speed from him, judging by all the goals I scored on the soccer pitch. Bravery I was yet to find out.

Each township has its own type of hustle. In KwaMashu, it is strictly robbery. In Chesterville, they have perfected the art of housebreaking. You buy the latest in home entertainment in Chesterville, at prices lower than low. In my township, Umlazi, we steal cars at such a rate that the flying squad—fly as they do—can never keep up.

"I know you are growing now."

We were in the Ford Courier, road-testing it. Not a drop of water had spilled during the coffee-cup test. I had been inside many cars—some turbo-charged, some with mind-blowing conversions. Different drivers too, but none of them handled a car like my father. He did not just drive the car, he tamed it, so that he could do whatever he wanted with it. Gears were changed with impeccable timing. When he had a manual-transmission Toyota Cressida—I was about ten—Dad changed gears so perfectly that the neighbors thought the transmission was automatic.

"And your generation is the fastest growing the ancestors have ever seen."

I liked it when my father spoke. His were words from a mind that sifts out all excess thoughts.

"You left school. I don't agree with your decision, but I see why you came to your conclusion. The world outside school is the real world. What I am about to tell you now I will never repeat again. Are you listening?"

"Yes, Dad," I said.

"You are now in the real world. In the real world, money matters. Notes are the tiny hands that spin this world around. The more of these tiny hands you have, the better your life will be. In this real world, you focus on what you want and go hard for it. You see school as an avenue to nowhere, but there are other ways to profit as well. Use your talents to gain. But you see this..."

Dad pulled his overall by the collar to reveal his tattooed shoulders. He looked straight into my eyes with regret all over his face.

"My boy, this is a man-made fairy tale. Don't believe in it. Whatever avenue you choose, don't make the mistake of taking this fairy tale to heart, or anything that will limit your thoughts. Boy, in this world you are born alone. Remember that. For every step you take, make sure you gauge your gain. Measure exactly how that step will help you. Life is progress, my boy. But for whatever you do, my son, put muthi first. For protection."

I had learned over the years not to interrupt him.

"What do you think goes on in the night? You think you roam the streets alone? As you walk, bad spirits are on your left and right, back and front."

I knew what would follow. And it did.

"You are going nowhere today. I have already arranged with old man Mbatha. He is expecting us."

From as far back in my seventeen years as scientists say memory begins, I had known old man Mbatha. He was our family's traditional healer. Despite what people will say, most township families have one. When doctors and their medicines failed, we went to old man Mbatha. With him it was always from the ground—trees and natural concoctions. The old man cured everything, from headaches to illnesses cosmic and emotional. Once, when Nu was five and had stopped talking, old man Mbatha cured her. He burned so much incense that Nu removed her thumb and coughed.

"It smells bad," she said, causing my mother to burst into a mixture of prayer and ululation.

"You are great, God," came from my mother's mouth, along with sweat from her brow and tears from her eyes.

"The child is only half cured," old man Mbatha said. "Your ancestors do not ask for much. Slaughter a goat, make sorghum beer."

It turned out to be a big party. My father got money from somewhere. The ancestors ate and drank a lot.

I had been to old man Mbatha's White Room three times in my life. The first time was when Nu regained the power of speech. The second time was after my car accident. Both times I took old man Mbatha's antics for granted. It was all like a big joke. All through those two visits I fought hard to contain my laughter. I did not believe that anyone could speak to the ancestors. That, in turn, made my father so angry he did not speak to me for two days straight.

The third time I was in the White Room, however, turned me into a true believer. Maybe the somber nature of my visit encouraged me to believe. I was at the lowest point in my life. When I was sixteen and a half, another soul departed from this world by my hand.

❖

The day my world turned black had started out a brilliant blue. Under a cool, cloudless morning sky my uncle Stan dropped off my cousin, Mandla, who was to spend the summer holidays with us. He was my favorite cousin, for the simple fact that although he had been to private school, he possessed no discernible traces of snobbery. Out of all his other cousins, some of whom lived in mansions, Mandla chose our house and my company for his holidays. We were more like brothers, and twins at that, for our age difference was mere hours.

I had saved for that whole year so we could avoid the frustrations of previous years, when we could only go to parties around my neighborhood because neither of us had a driver's license. We drank ourselves to sleep in the backyard, annoyed because Mandla had invitations to almost all the suburban parties, but we were not able to attend. This will be our year, I told myself every time I banked under my mattress. When my cash stash reached R1500, I bought a driver's license in B Section. The man who sold licenses met me on the street. I gave him two passport photos. Two days later, I gave him the money upon receipt of the license.

A week before he arrived, Mandla had set out the schedule for the weekend. First on the itinerary, on Friday, was a party organized by his schoolmates in Woodlands. We would hit the city on Saturday for a night of club-hopping. The day I got my license, my father gave me the keys to one of the old scraps rotting in our backyard. It passed the coffee-cup test just hours before Mandla arrived.

We partied in Woodlands with Mandla's schoolmates until the early hours. Although he was drunk from early on in the afternoon, Mandla was cozy with his girlfriend from school for most of the night. I enjoyed their hassle-free mode of partying and the openness with which the girls talked to me—none of the discrimination of township girls, for whom reputations were paramount. They never gave this bush mechanic a chance. In the township, only the car thieves and working guys were given the time of day—lots of it.

To this day, I regret rolling the blunt that meant I left the party to smoke by the car on the road outside the yard. Most of all, I regret that I dozed off.

Frantic bangs on the driver's window of the old car. "He is killing Mandla! Help him, help him!"

Mandla's girl nearly broke the window. She was crying. Her face looked like she was in excruciating physical pain.

I turned to look at the back of the car, where her hand was pointing, but saw nothing. When I got out, I saw Mandla taking a serious beating from a much older man on the grass behind the car. He sat astride Mandla and punched away. As I neared, he pulled out a knife.

"Don't kill him!" I shouted.

Mandla held up his arms to protect his face. The man planted the knife in his forearm, but Mandla mustered his strength and wriggled free. The man went after him. I heard the force of the knife as it gashed Mandla's back. He fell face down in the middle of the road. The man wasn't finished, and he began kicking and stomping on Mandla. I went for the spanner in the boot of my car. When I saw blood gush from Mandla's forehead, nose, arm and back, it was as if a veil had fallen over my eyes. I saw Mandla crying and his girl screaming. I saw the man standing over Mandla and cursing. Yet I heard nothing—the veil over my eyes was accompanied by eerie silence. But I heard the man's skull crack as I landed blow after solid blow with the wheel spanner. We left him there—eyes open, unconscious, his right leg twitching violently.

I regained my hearing at Addington Hospital. The nurses cleaned Mandla's wounds and stitched him up. His girl went with us.

"What were they fighting about?" I asked her as we sat on a bench in the casualty ward.

"That man grabbed me. He tried to take me by force. He was gatecrashing—no one knows him. He nearly killed Mandla. Mandla nearly died for me."

That night the three of us slept in the old car in the

YOUNG BLOOD

hospital parking lot.

I woke first and turned to the back seat, to Mandla asleep and his bandaged arm and broken nose and understood that it was not a dream. His girl was next to him, eyes open and red like she had not slept. I shared a cigarette with her on the beach sand.

"You are covered. The people we left at the party called while you were asleep. The police believed the story my friends made up. They heard a noise and saw the man lying on the road. You are covered," she said.

"But the guy can press charges. This is far from over," I said. She held my hand but turned her face away.

"Paramedics pronounced him dead on the scene. You are covered. Mandla is awake. Can you drop me at the New Germany taxi rank?"

It was my turn to look away.

"We will, but give me a minute. I'll come to the car in a second. I need to wash my face," I said.

I shed tears for the dead man. I saw myself on the horizon—all across the sky it was definitely me, aged seven, waving goodbye. Mandla left that afternoon to convalesce in Pietermaritzburg.

"He was killing Mandla, Dad. He was killing him. Please don't tell Ma," I sobbed when I told my father. He put his hand on my shoulder.

"You must see old man Mbatha. I feel so sorry for you, my boy. You do not deserve a baptism of such flames. But this will pass; believe me when I tell you it will pass. You must see old man Mbatha—he will facilitate your apologies to the dead man."

In beach sand at Port Edward, I dug a hole two

meters deep. At the bottom I laid the murder weapon and a liter of sorghum beer. Old man Mbatha held a live black goat by his side. He looked out to sea. Apologies to the dead man rolled off his tongue as rapid orations. I laid the goat at the bottom of the hole. Old man Mbatha pricked my finger for a drop of blood. As soon as my blood made contact with the goat, old man Mbatha instructed me to bury it alive. "Do it fast. When you finish, make sure you do not look back. Otherwise all of this will be in vain," he said.

I struggled, but resisted the urge to look back. On the way back to the township, after an hour of silence, I started to nod off. I felt old man Mbatha's cold hand on my shoulder.

"The fire is still there, boy, just burning slower. Your ancestors say keep it this way," he said.

I stayed with old man Mbatha for seven days. At the end of that week he proclaimed the apology accepted. I believed this wholeheartedly, for never once did I meet the dead man in a nightmare. That alone was proof enough.

❖

The White Room was at the back of old man Mbatha's house. I went in alone; my father stayed on the bench outside. On entering, I left my shoes at the door. Old man Mbatha was clad in a red-and-black cloak. Small black-and-white beaded ornaments adorned his neck and wrists. He stood in the middle of the room, head bowed. He motioned me to sit in front of him. A weak incense—much weaker than what had made Nu talk—was set alight.

"Call your ancestors and state your business," he said.

I called them all, pitch perfect, the way my father taught me. Old man Mbatha sat down. He looked at the floor; his whole body rested on his left hand for balance. His head slanted left, like that of a weeping widow at a wake. Black women sit like this when they are forlorn or defeated.

"I am going into the world." I stated my business.

"What is it you want from the world?"

My father once told me that people like old man Mbatha know what you want before you say it. That day he assumed nothing.

"Money," I said.

"Very well, boy. Let me talk to your ancestors, to see what they say." To talk to my ancestors, old man Mbatha went into a corner. There, head bowed, he looked up and whistled. The corner whistled back. This conversation in whistles lasted for nearly eight minutes. There were points when it became heated; he and the wall whistled simultaneously, like when an argument comes close to boiling point.

The conversation of whistles ended and he turned to face me. For a second before he bowed his head again, I saw that his eyes were bloodshot. Deep concern sat on his face. He regained his composure, assumed the weeping-widow posture, and spoke.

"Your ancestors say, do what you must do but know where you are going. They will not protect you unnecessarily."

He wrapped my medication—tree bark and roots—in newspapers. Roots to boil in water, allow to cool, then drink.

"One liter of this will do," he said.

Tree bark to boil in water, sift, drink until the stomach takes no more, then induce vomiting.

"Drink five liters of this one—not less. Take both morning and night until all is finished. You will pay me a quarter of the first money you make and no more."

On the way home I began to tell my father what old man Mbatha had told me. My father looked at me.

"I do not need to know," he said. "Boy, it is your secret."

❖

Of the twelve houses in my street, only two had father figures. Most of my friends in 2524 Close grew up without fathers. When fights broke out over the things boys fight over, mothers resolved the scuffles with angry shouts from their kitchen half-doors: "Carry on with the nonsense you are pulling. We will see. Your fighting will take you to jail or six feet under. We will see."

The other father in 2524 Close was Mr. Mthembu, or Mthombeni, Mthalane, Mtheku, or something like that. I never saw him much because he worked shifts at Toyota in Prospecton. His house was the only one in the street with DSTV.

I had Dad at home. I was glad there was a man who told me something about life, who put his hand on my shoulder when I took a life and told me the hurt would pass. Who drilled me on engines so I could also eat. Who showed me the stars on his shoulders and told me "never." In his few words, Dad told me all he knew and left out all he wished he never knew.

When I thought I was at a dead end, my father took me to a man who told me I would get what I wanted. Dad told me I was in the real world. Money is what I wanted from the real world. My father told me something about life, at least. Most of the people I knew never had this privilege. When Dad told me he did not need to know what old man Mbatha had told me, it was another lesson in the real world. A man keeps his secrets.

SiBANi
MEANS LiGHT

I Only Saw Gunfire was on old man Mbatha's treatment for six days. It was with a sense of relief that I boiled the last of the roots and tree bark.

The roots caused no problems—the liter I drank actually made me feel stronger. My problem was with the boiled tree bark: it was bitter on the palate and the sheer volume of liquid I took in was unbearable. Even worse was the vomiting; every time it came out, my face felt like it was exploding.

My father added more muthi to my treatment— minty leaves that I boiled and steamed over while completely naked. I called those leaves my "lung cleaner sauna," because after each session my chest opened up considerably, something I had last felt when I was serious about soccer, in the time before cigarettes and weed.

A ban on alcohol and sex was in force during the treatment. Old man Mbatha had placed the ban but my father enforced it with vigor. His stare locked on to me even when I went to the shops for airtime for my cellphone. I felt healthy, though; that aspect of the treatment I did not fault. Every day I woke with freaky freshness. There was also a lot of time on my hands, which I spent with my father under cars in the backyard.

Musa was delighted when I told him about my trip to old man Mbatha and the treatment. He passed by every night with weed for me and beer for himself. The lung cleaner sauna rejuvenated my lungs. They became strong again. I smoked weed without end.

"Do you have the list yet?" Vusi called one morning, a day before I bade farewell to the rigors of my treatment.

"No, Vusi," I said.

"This is not good. We can only make cash if we move fast, or am I the only one who thinks this way?"

"You are telling the wrong person. Call Musa and tell him."

"I doubt if he is serious about this. Maybe he will listen to you, because every time I call him, he says he will get the list soon."

"If he says so, maybe soon is not that far away."

"It is the way he says it, Sipho."

"How does he say it?"

"So laid back I'm beginning to doubt if the list even exists."

Musa came by later that night. In clouds of weed smoke, by the blue wall, I told him about Vusi's call but delicately left out all the parts about doubt.

"Vusi must learn to calm down. I told him he will know when we have the list. I don't know what he called you for. He is overeager. We will get the list when you are done with your treatment. I just hope he did like you did. Most of these young crooks today don't believe in muthi, even though it works. That is one thing I learned in prison—muthi works. I saw people walk free from certain conviction because of it," Musa said.

"Muthi? How do people get it in jail?"

"Money. You can get anything into jail if you have money. You will be surprised the things you can get in jail with money. In our cell we had a TV and DVD player. We even had a cellphone. There is a whole other world behind those walls, Sipho. It has its own rules and economy. Food is cheap—you get a whole chicken for R5—but drugs are more expensive than on the outside."

"What were you in for?" I said.

"I pulled nine months for car theft."

Blitzed by the blunt, Musa told me about his nine months in prison. He left for Joburg because the other shoplifters told him things were better there. For three months they really were. His graduation from shoplifter to car thief came within two months. As the perennial all-rounder, Musa excelled at car theft. By the third month in Joburg, he was working exclusively for a syndicate headed by Sibani. At the end of the third month, Musa was arrested in a stolen car. He never squealed about the syndicate. This raised his profile in Sibani's eyes.

Welcomed with open arms by Sibani's connections in jail, Musa kept his mouth shut and absorbed the rules of the prison world. Only money really mattered, and the quickest brain was always the winner. Sibani sent him a weekly allowance of R100, the notes stuffed in a loaf of bread and delivered by a different person each time.

It was no coincidence that Musa was placed in a cell with associates of Sibani. Everything is paid for in prison.

"What made you take the number?" I said.

"I did not so much take it, it was given to me. This old man who controlled the cell, Sibani's friend, ran a tight ship. He sold weed. As a top 26 old-timer, he ruled the cell and indeed the whole gang. The day I got my medal was one of those days when jail really feels like jail. The 26s went on a stabbing spree in the kitchen. The old-timer gave the order because someone else was selling weed, and worse, he was a 28. On days like those in prison, when the gangs are at each other, that is when you see that you are actually in hell. The guards lock the doors and go home. Prisoners are left to themselves.

"The 28s retaliated. It went on through the night. A lot of people died that day. The corridors smelled of blood. The war went on until the early hours of the morning. In our cell, all the soldiers—the lowest rank in the gang—were out fighting on all fronts. The old man gave instructions to his two generals, who relayed these to four captains, who rushed out of the cell to tell the soldiers.

"So I am sitting on my bed in the corner—me and two other guys in the cell—when four 28s enter and head straight for the old-timer. Everyone froze, even the generals. The old-timer ran to our corner, pulled out two knives, and looked straight into my eyes. The 28s meant business; they had already disemboweled the two generals. The old-timer gave me a knife and told me to stab them. And we did.

"That is how I became a 26 general. It was just spontaneous survival instinct. I stabbed until my hands trembled, then I stabbed some more. I don't want to talk about it anymore, Sipho. Everytime I think about it, the wind smells like blood."

❖

I was with Musa in the township of Chesterville when Sibani called. Musa was giving me a practical lecture on one of his many ways of making pocket money. It was the simplest of plans, really. He gave me R500, and we went to the Mandrax merchant's house in Chesterville.

The love affair between Mandrax fiends and housebreaking is age old. There is nothing more un-reliable than a Mandrax fiend, except perhaps Durban December weather. These boys will say, their mouths dry and cracking white, "We got this from the sub-urbs." Their cravings lead them to steal even from neighboring houses in their townships. The risk is tenfold in the townships, though. If they steal from the poor and get caught, death is usually sudden.

Musa bought a DVD player and a digital camera for R700. I bought a four-component music system for R500. Then we went to the university up in Westville and opened shop. Musa made a R1000 profit. I sold the music system for R1500. I returned Musa's R500. As we headed to the city to see Sibani, R1000 was in my back pocket—the quickest pocket money I ever made.

We were to find Sibani at the student flats that make up most of what is upper Berea. The flats house students from various tertiary institutions around Durban. Upper Berea was often hectic, but more so on a month-end Friday. The Musgrave Center up the road, the Durban University of Technology down the hill. It depended on your mood, really: working girls drunk at the mall, or tertiary girls weeded and drunk at DUT.

"I've got to see this list," Musa said, and looked at his arm to verify the flat number.

There was no answer on the intercom, but the gate opened. The door to the flat was unlocked. We were greeted by a cloud of weed smoke.

Through the cloud I made out two girls in their late teens on either side of a light-skinned man in his mid-twenties. They were sharing a blunt on a couch so low it looked like it was built for children. When the cloud shifted, I saw that the girls were even lighter in complexion than the man.

"Sibani, how are you, my brother?" Musa shook Sibani's hand.

"All right, my brother, but where are your manners? You did not greet my friends."

The peach-skinned girls, converted to shyness by Sibani's comment, or perhaps by the weed, stood up to hug Musa. I was right behind him and felt warmth and weed and perfume when it was my turn for a hug.

I could not help but stare as the girls crisscrossed the room in search of beanbag chairs for us to sit on. Striking in their jeans and T-shirts, their features seemed flawless to me. Either they were not aware of their beauty or were comfortable enough in that real-ization that it had set deep inside and did not need to be expressed. As students, they were easy to talk to. In a few years, they would be unapproachable. We had caught them in the middle of a smoke fest. The beanbags offered to Musa and me were uncomfort-able, the padding all but gone. The wooden floor of the flat had once been elegant but was now just old. The walls were adorned with a large Lauryn Hill poster and smaller posters of celebrities unknown to me. We waited for Mdala, a friend of Sibani's, who was out buying food. In the time we were there, I fell in love twice with each of the girls, three times with the girl who had thick, almost black lips. I can't help it—I love upcountry girls, with their shy eyes and slangless speech.

The ashtray was on the couch between Sibani's thighs. I had never seen him up close before. Usually, his M5 was parked at the R Section garage while he talked business with the shady owner, or else it was a shiny black blur speeding past on the freeway. Without an ounce of jealousy in me, I can state that Sibani was a man so handsome he bordered on pretty. I silently wondered—as blunts passed from hand to hand in a cloud of smoke—how he schemed with battle-scarred crooks. How did they take him seriously, with his unblemished skin and male-model features?

"I have the list at home, boys, and it is juicy. Half of it reads Beemer, the other half reads Benz."

Sibani tilted his head upwards, spoke, and exhaled weed smoke at the same time.

"We need to see it," Musa said when one of the three burning blunts was passed to him. "We really need to see it, Sibani. We have to start."

"That is why I did not want anyone else but you on this, Musa. I like your drive, Mr. Do It Now. Mdala will be back soon. In the meantime, let's puff some more."

Sibani passed the blunt.

Sure enough, Mdala returned, but only after an

hour. Highly weeded, I rode with him in Sibani's M5. To my disappointment, Mdala did not pump the fire pedal hard enough on the beast.

Musa and Sibani trailed us by a kilometer or so in the 325is. On the freeway to Pinetown, Mdala let it rip a bit. His expression loosened. "Sibani tells me you boys will be working soon. Play this well and you will never be poor. Don't roll with the clowns; always remember it is money you want. This will help you avoid trouble most times," he said.

He also told me he knew my father from way back. And, more interestingly, that he desperately wanted a manual-transmission six-speed BMW 540i.

Mdala's life was the kind that we looked at from a distance and instantly envied. On the other side of fifty, but a decade younger in the looks department, Mdala was a BMW specialist. He knew every secret— for a car is made in layers—on every BMW built after 1980. I'd sometimes see him tearing up the township in his matchbox BMW 535i. It was Avus blue, a sublime acoustic bastard that walked on BBS rims. I once saw him take apart a BMW engine and put it back together—drunk—with indifferent ease. In dress, Mdala was old school, with formal shirts, creased trousers and shiny shoes. In the game of money, though, he was post-future school. He owned two mansions in the township. His taxis always looked new. Mdala was what we in the township call a "razo"—a classic old-timer rider. Sibani lived in Kloof, in a symmetrical, white-pillared hideaway that resembled a corporate office. The lighting outside made it appear bluish, like a glacier I once saw in a school geography book. In the lounge, the lights were in such awkward places I wondered how the light bulbs were changed.

We poured whiskies. Sibani placed the list on the table.

"It is up to you which one you start with. There are ten in all and we have two months, not more," he said.

Sibani and Mdala were similar—formal dress code and zero slang in speech. Calm too, like that hour immediately after midnight in the township.

Sibani did not give us the original list. Instead, he gave us a page torn from an exercise book, the childish writing showing a strong Model C influence—the i's had round balls over them. As I scanned the list, I was between BMW 735i and Mercedes-Benz E320 when I caught sight of the writer. She was maybe seven years old. In her right hand she held a creamy, velvety teddy bear. Not to be outdone, a bright orange Winnie the Pooh was on her left arm. She was in the passageway leading to the lounge, oblivious of us all. Her stare across the room to Sibani brought a pause to the proceedings. "Do you see my baby girl, Musa?" Sibani said as he moved toward the child.

The question was addressed to Musa, but was in fact for all of us. Then she turned Sibani into a child.

"Why are you not sleeping?" I heard Sibani ask as he lifted the girl.

"I'm not drowsy. Ma said we are going to the beach tomorrow. In school we..."

And they faded into the passageway, to whatever luxuries lay beyond, to a wife and mother I never saw.

Sibani was busy with family matters for a good hour or so. We killed time with a soccer match on TV. For most of the first half, Mdala slept—the only clue to his age. He looked close to fifty in my eyes, but with his facial muscles relaxed, sleep added five more years to my estimate. Sibani reappeared wearing pajamas, a silk robe and flip-flops.

"Wake up, old man." He shook Mdala.

"It is this boring soccer game. Let's go to KwaMashu, I need to see a friend there who promised me whiskey," Mdala said.

We hurried our drinks. I was surprised when Sibani also came along.

"Change clothes, at least," Mdala said on the driveway outside.

"I can't change again. The wife will think I'm up to no good. This way, she will think I will be back soon."

Sibani closed the passenger door of the 325is.

Then they did two things wrong. The first was letting me drive Sibani's M5. I fell in love with that car. When I clocked that matchbox M5 it freed my heart. An engine so powerful and fast—with the windows down it really felt like flight. Mdala was in the passenger seat next to me, and there was a smile on his face the whole time. As we mazed away from Kloof, it felt like raw sex in stops and starts. Still, I let the machine rip so many times it seemed like the freeway would never come. When the rev counter kissed red, I changed it up. It sang music to my heart.

I cooled it down when we entered KwaMashu, the streets busy like it was broad daylight. Mdala knocked on the door of a friend's house. Through the rear-view mirror I saw Musa and Sibani sitting in the 325is.

A yellow BMW parked next to Musa's 325is. Barry White—the CD was Mdala's—made it hard for me to hear what was said. Sibani went to the driver's side of the yellow BMW. Mdala opened the door to his friend's house. In the rear-view mirror, I saw Sibani pull a silver .45 pistol from the pocket of his robe. He placed the pistol against the temple of the driver of the yellow BMW. I blinked once and Sibani was on bullet number two—the man's head gushed blood, his body instantly slumped. Sibani unloaded the entire magazine of the .45. His silk robe obeyed the wind as he ran to the passenger seat of the M5.

Cool as ice, Sibani looked at me. "Let's go. Clock it again," he said.

The second reason it was wrong for me to drive the M5 was that it was the getaway car. As we left the township, it was like riding a fire-breathing dragon—way more exhilarating than just racing.

WE MOVED WITH EASE DOWN THE SOUTH COAST

I don't remember the speedometer and rev counter. The gauges on the dashboard ceased to exist for the moment. All I recall is the car and the road.

Sibani leaned his seat back as far as it would go. He sank into it and relaxed while I gave the M5 my best. The pistol lay in his lap. When I clocked the M5 in lower gears, I saw sparks in the rear-view mirror as the tow bar kissed the road. The tires left marks on every bend and corner we took. Outside KwaMashu, Sibani called Musa on his cellphone.

"We'll meet up at my Pinetown house. Is Mdala with you? Okay, let's meet up in Pinetown," Sibani said.

I shoved the M5 as hard as I could. On the freeway to Pinetown the accelerator pedal locked onto the floor. The sound from the tailpipe was like gunfire as the engine clocked again and again. Sibani forced an indifferent smile that made him look like a posing male model. I tapped the pedal once; on release, the M5 went into super-drive—like in video games when a car is injected with nitrous oxide.

In Pinetown, Sibani pointed the way with his pistol. He waited until I was so close to each turn that it was almost impossible to negotiate. Then he pointed the way. For every corner, I used the handbrake to turn, which left more marks on the road. This amused Sibani; his smile grew wider. The wider he grinned, the more terrifying he looked. My only wish was to keep turning left—that way, his pistol did not point in my direction. My father once told me that the barrel of a gun pointed in your direction brings bad luck, whether the gun is loaded or not.

"Slow down after the second house on your left; the mechanism on my gate is slow. Don't damage it; it was fitted only two days ago." Sibani reached into the pocket of his robe. He retrieved a small remote control and pressed it. The shiny steel gate glided slowly, as if it sat on the shell of a moving snail. My heartbeat rang loud in my brain, as if my heart had somehow relocated to my head. My forearms were wet, like I had dipped them in water. We had not stopped since the hit in KwaMashu.

"You can shove a car, Sipho; I will give you that. But you are sweating all over my seats. Are you sick or something?"

"No, Sibani, it is this heat. It is hot tonight."

"You need to see a doctor to check you out, because this is the coldest night we've had this year. It looks like winter is finally here."

"Maybe it is the treatment I was on. I only finished it today; maybe it is still in my system."

Sibani was on a call before I had finished my explanation. I doubt if he really wanted to hear one. I checked myself in the rear-view mirror. Sweat on my brow and nose, even behind my ears. I drove through the gate as soon as the gap was wide enough for the car.

I eased the M5 down a recently tarred driveway. The house was new. It sat in a flat, barren yard, enclosed by a high plastered wall crowned with electrified wires. The house itself was coarsely plastered. I parked in front of the double garage.

Sibani jumped out of the passenger seat to open one of the roller doors. He motioned with his pistol to the parking place. Stacked bags of cement were proof that the house was a work in progress. I got out and placed my hand on the bonnet of the M5, but quickly recoiled because it was burning hot. The twin tailpipes—cleansed by speed—were ashy white. Sibani closed the roller door from the inside. As we exited through a side door, I heard the 325is in violent change-downs on the driveway. A light, chilly wind nearly knocked me out. I directed all the strength I had to my legs.

"Do you have glasses in the house?"

Mdala had a bottle of Glenfiddich in his hand. He left the door of the 325is ajar.

"You like to make me look like a drunk, old man. The house is not even finished—no furniture—but you expect me to have glasses. You are really getting old, Mdala," Sibani said.

"And you as a drunk should have a glass for me—if not in the house maybe in your car. Otherwise, why are we here?"

"You are my ride home," Sibani smiled.

In the 325is, Musa laughed uncontrollably.

"We'll buy a tumbler at a garage, old man," Musa shouted through chuckles.

Mdala refused to drink whiskey in a tumbler, so we

went over to Sibani's Kloof house. My heart started its slow descent back to my ribcage. The cold air turned my sweat into minute, shiny salt crystals—light white dust on my palms. My eyes were out the back window of the 325is all the way to Kloof, but I don't recall a thing I saw. I was overcome by a feeling of unease as we downed whiskey in silence at Sibani's house. In the township, we grow up around killers, so there is really nothing I fear. I had seen murders before, and even taken life myself. But those thirty minutes at Sibani's house, after he had emptied the magazine of a .45 pistol into a man's head, filled every cell in my body with dread. I looked at Sibani in a different light. When I realized I had killed a man, I lost my mind completely. But Sibani was enjoying every moment of it. In those minutes, he really scared me. He was quiet, but his face had a look almost of joy.

With the whiskey just below the shoulder of the bottle, Musa got a call. We had to leave for the city. We left Mdala and Sibani in Kloof—Mdala sprawled awkwardly on a couch, Sibani's satisfied mug glued to the muted plasma TV.

It was as if Musa knew exactly how I felt; after the hit in KwaMashu and the getaway to Pinetown, I did not need speed. My friend was gentle on the 325is; he kept it below 100 km/h. We parked outside a flat in North Beach in the city.

Musa was in the flats for slightly over an hour. All the CDs in his stereo were upbeat house music. But there was nothing to be happy about. I opted for the tuner instead. It was not long before I switched the stereo off—every song sounded like a scream.

I leaned on the front fender of the 325is and took

brisk drags of a cigarette in the cool, fresh air. The wind had turned chilly. I got inside the car. In the silence of the passenger seat, I caught my reflection in the side mirror. Worry engulfed my face. I tried hard but failed to force a smile. I thought about Sibani, watching a muted soccer match on TV, satisfied like he had just made love to the most beautiful woman on earth. And Mdala, taking yet another nap. And Musa, who carried on as if nothing had happened. He came out of the flats fresh, like it was morning.

"Let's check out which clubs are popping. There's a beautiful girl I want you to meet at DUT," he said.

"No, Musa, take me home. I'm drowsy and my stomach is acting up."

"Are you sure? She smokes; you should see her. Hourglass figure with plenty of ass."

"I can't. I don't want to spoil your night. Take me home where I can shit in peace."

Musa knew exactly how I felt, and did not press on the club idea. On the freeway to the township we shared a blunt.

"What is the story with your friend? Is Sibani mad or something? What was all that about?" I said.

"If only you knew the story, Sipho. The snake Sibani killed was a police informant. You know, the fakes that pretend they are hustlers but they work with the law. Snakes, Sipho. He dropped Sibani's name to a detective we know. Only last week Sibani sold three taxis to the same detective. There was no way he wouldn't tip off Sibani. Everything goes smooth without the snakes. I commend Sibani, I commend the detective and I commend you for a smooth getaway. The world is better without snakes," Musa said.

We did not chill by the blue wall. I jumped out of the 325is before Musa had even pulled the hand-brake. I rushed inside, pretending to attend to a runny stomach. I tiptoed to my room, pulled the covers over myself and fell asleep fully dressed.

❖

I woke to a red dawn. I smoked endless cigarettes, watching the sun turn deep gold, then silver. For the remainder of the day, police helicopters hovered over the townships. They were looking for the M5. Musa's contacts from Chesterville and Lamontville confirmed this over the phone. Mdala's friend from KwaMashu was not pleased: Sibani had pulled a hit virtually on his front doorstep. But Mdala explained to him that the killing had to happen. Bullets had to right a wrong.

At half-hourly intervals, police helicopters hovered overhead. Right on cue, the cars of the flying squad glided by. They found no M5. They did this even when they were looking for stolen vehicles. They must have thought we were really stupid. They did not find these cars parked on the streets. Instead of investigating, they just looked.

My father and Ma left with Nu for Howick early that morning. Uncle Stan had given Ma a voucher for a weekend getaway to some resort. Ma knew I would decline the offer; she hadn't even asked me to join them.

I bought a plastic coin bag of weed from Mama Mkhize. Parts of the movie from the previous night starring Sibani had to be edited out. On top of that, Mama Mkhize's words baffled me.

"Don't worry about it, Sipho. Some of these boys think they run the show. These things are done because it has to be so," she said.

It amazed me how fast news traveled in crime circles. I was the latest arrival, a newborn in the world of cold words and frozen actions.

I called Vusi for a chillout. Of course, he needed to see the list.

It was close to midday when Vusi parked outside the blue wall. He was driving a red Fiat Uno. The last time I saw him—at the beach, when Musa laid out the plan—Vusi had been driving an Opel Kadett GSI. I motioned him to park inside since I was home alone. He was eager, and when I gave him the list, I swear he got the chills. That only lasted a second; just as quickly he wore a mask of disbelief and excitement in equilibrium. He shook his head as he read the list. At the back of the house, he made little ticks on the list. A tick meant he knew where to find the car.

"I know exact locations and the best times to get them," he said. People live their lives mostly with doubt as to their purpose in life. In Vusi I saw one of the very few who knew what he was in this world for. Stealing cars was his thing. He chose to live that way, or that way chose his life—that can happen too. It is madness where we live. No matter who did the choosing, Vusi lived his life with stoic calm. It was evident even in the way he answered his phone, taking it smoothly and silently from his pocket. He ticked the list eight times, with no sound of pen on paper.

"You know, Sipho, if we are serious about this we can go even now. I know a dolphin-shaped BMW

535i at Amanzimtoti. Unless we move, nothing will happen. Let's get this money, bro. Just think, Sipho, in a few hours you will have a couple of thousands. This smoking won't bring the car to us. Let's go," he said.

We picked up Vusi's sister, Mimi, from a hair salon in B Section. She was to drop us off at Amanzimtoti and return to the township in the Fiat Uno. A twinkle shimmered over Mimi, indicating she was crossing the border from girlhood to womanhood. But she drove like a man. She spoke only once, and that was to defend R&B music. We said it was lying to us, a misleading fantasy. She said, for her, fantasy was better than reality any time of the day. Her words were a honeyed cameo. For the remainder of the outing, she was quiet and nearly floored the Uno. We talked about music, told a joke or two and tried hard to be relaxed. Yet the hooves of a thousand horses were pounding out a beat in my chest.

The 535i was in the suburban part of Amanzimtoti, a distant scream from my grandmother's house on the dusty fringes of the same area. The target was outside a restaurant called Oasis, whose claim to fame was that it was the only restaurant in the province made of timber logs. The balcony upstairs looked out onto the Amanzimtoti River as it fed into the Indian Ocean. We drove past it once. Mimi dropped us next to a petrol station a short distance from the restaurant.

The 535i hugged the fourth parking space to the right of the downstairs entrance. First, I was the lookout man while Vusi worked on the driver's side of the maroon-colored beast. Then I became a patron about to enter: I checked my pockets, waited to butt

YOUNG BLOOD

a cigarette, talked as if at the end of a cellphone conversation. Then I checked for my wallet and absorbed the view. The people inside carried on eating and drinking. Until Vusi started the car I did not hear a sound, and I was close. If you have ever seen a car thief at work—and you probably never have—the only word to describe it is "swift."

When in a stolen car driven by a nut like Vusi, fasten your seat belt and stay calm. Never tell him to tone it down unless you want it full throttle. Not that there is anything wrong with speed. It's just a personal matter—I like it only when I'm the one driving. The dolphin-shaped BMW 535i was no matchbox M5, but it glided almost as well. Vusi was next to me, accelerator pedal to the floor, calm like a Sunday morning.

A couple of minutes into our getaway, we stopped at one of the many gravel roads that fern the main road in KwaMakhutha. I felt the hooves in my chest weaken. Eventually, when I slept, it was as if just one stud was left. I checked the car. It did not have an anti-hijack system.

We parked the car in Vusi's cramped backyard under an improvised carport and covered it. The car's tailpipe was hot and white, the bonnet warm. We took what we could—a digital camera, a plastic bag with three types of cheese, two PlayStation 2 joysticks, a fancy silver pen and R317 from the ashtray. When Vusi suggested we go to the city, I opted for a night alone at home.

"I'll let you drive next time. You will feel the thrill," he said. We shared a cigarette by the blue wall.

"What's next on the list?" I said.

"I'll tell you in the morning when we split the money," Vusi replied.

I took a shower but still felt fucked up. It did not help that I quickly smoked two blunts from Vusi's dark green stash. I fell into a dreamy state, my mind alternating between too fast and too slow. My cellphone was out of airtime. I was already living inside a blur when I went to the drawer where Ma hid the telephone key. I unlocked the phone and called Nana.

I fell asleep on the dining room sofa, phone receiver in my hand, the TV watching me.

MY FIRST CAR

The blare of the TV and hunger pains woke me in the morning. My body felt fresh, my mind clear. I took a shower first—a ritual Ma had drilled into me back in childhood and which I voluntarily embraced into my teenage years. Break the fast clean.

The bathroom mirror revealed a less worried reflection. I smiled and looked closely at the eyes. Just like mine, the skin folded at the borders of the lids. As I got dressed in my room, the same eyes threw back a judgmental gaze.

In the kitchen, I made scrambled eggs and poured orange juice. I ate breakfast to SABC Africa news. Civil wars, floods, refugees, men with fat heads shaking hands. Mud huts in desert wastelands, a machete-wielding mob hacking a man to death. A message on my phone switched my focus to the day ahead. Vusi and my cut of the money, the mouthful of pride I needed to swallow so I could apologize to Nana. I missed her.

I retrieved the message, hoping it was from Vusi. The sender was Nana: "Baby I know u said it will b a surprise but give me a hint of what to wear—casual or formal. Don't want 2 look out of place. Kisses, luv u," it read.

I remembered that I had called her, but was at a loss as to what we had talked about. The call I was so eager for followed soon after. Vusi sounded curt over loud music.

"You at home?"

"Yes," I said.

"I'll be there in thirty minutes."

I washed the pan, glass and plate. In the backyard I sat on blocks left over from the construction of the blue wall. Over a morning cigarette my gaze locked on the shacks of Power. The usual morning cloud of dust rose over the shantytown; the whole neighborhood seemed to spew dust in unison. I give nothing but respect to the women of Power: every morning, without fail, they wake to sweep their dusty yards.

On bricks next to me stood the remnants of the car I had driven the day I killed Mandla's attacker. My father had sold it in pieces; the engine was first to go. Doors, fenders and seats followed. The chassis proved harder to sell. Oxidation spread rapidly, engulfing the whole thing in no time. It moves like HIV, my father once quipped of rust. My mind took an aimless stroll. Musa, Sibani, Mdala, Vusi, women of Power, the man whose life I took. Did he really forgive me? Nana. The horn of Vusi's car put an end to these thoughts. In my fingers, my morning cigarette was only ash—smoked almost entirely by the wind while my mind roamed. I took a lip-burning drag from what was left, puzzled by three girls who ran toward me through the gap in the blue wall.

"Vusi is calling you on the road. Sorry I did not greet. Can we use your toilet? Emergency."

"It is the green door next to the kitchen," I said. They continued their run into the house.

Vusi was sitting on a cooler box by the side of his Fiat Uno. He stood up to shake my hand, placed a glass on the roof of his car and urinated over the back tire.

"Howzit, Sipho, you look fresh. You really did sleep in. I thought you were drifting me when I left you here. The city is rotten—the tales I have of last night, bro, I tell you. You'd wish you were there."

"Where were you wilding out? Are you trying to break records? Three chicks for only one you?"

Vusi sat down on the cooler box. For his night out, white had been the color of choice. New white Jack Purcell tennis shoes, white black-label Hugo Boss jeans and plain white Armani T-shirt.

"I'm looking at you with yesterday's eyes. Do you want anything to drink? I have beer and cider. The city is rotten, my brother. Don't say you have a girlfriend if she clubs. They wild out so much. I wonder, bro, if it was meant to be this easy."

"Was Musa with you?"

"Sure, he gave me your cut. He was with girls from out of town—Tongaat, Stanger, or something. Here is your share. It should be R2 000."

I folded the notes into my pocket.

"Count it, Sipho. Make sure it is all there," Vusi said.

I unfolded the notes in my hand, counted a quick twenty. "What is your story? What are you up to today? Don't you drink anymore? I have beer and ciders."

"I'll drink later. What I need is a car. I think I prom-ised my girlfriend a date. I need to go see her at least just to find out what I said."

"You can use my Opel, but put petrol in it. At the least, it must return with the same amount it left with. We can fetch it at D Section."

"Vusi, do you have airtime? I want to send a message." I wrote "Casual, luv u 2" and sent the message to Nana. The trio was in the lounge with their shoes off.

"Don't relax, sisters, we are off to D Section," I said in passing.

In my room, under the mattress, I banked R1 000. I overheard half-hearted complaints bounce between the trio.

"Does Vusi ever sleep or just chill at least?"

"We danced on almost all the dance floors in the city. My feet are burning."

"You heard what he said, friend. He wants to vibe with us until we can vibe no more."

We all squeezed into the Fiat Uno. All three girls were quick to open and sip ciders, which stained their mouths. When Vusi made the introductions I almost laughed at their cherry tongues.

"I'm hungry, Sipho. Can we start at the J Section shops? They have fresh meat there," Vusi said.

He changed the seating arrangement. I became the driver; next to me sat one girl. In the back seat, Vusi was the meat in the sandwich. At the shops in J Section I bought two recharge vouchers. I sent Nana one recharge PIN and called her.

"Hey, baby, did you sleep well?"

"Yes, because the last voice I heard was yours."

"Say, baby, when do you think you will be ready?"

"Ma is making me clean the kitchen—say three

hours. But I'll call if I finish earlier. Thanks for the airtime, baby. Please tell me where we are going?"

I let the suspense linger.

"Call when you are ready then, baby."

We prepared the meat over an open fire at the shops in J Section but ate it in D Section.

We blunted in the backyard in D Section, after the meal of meat, bread and tomatoes. The trio dragged one puff each, proclaimed Vusi's stash way too potent and retired to the lounge.

"The house belongs to my uncle Sazi. He used to throw the wildest parties here. I lost my virginity in one of the rooms inside. He stays with us now, a shadow of himself. I'll tell you something about this HIV, my friend: it hinders progress. I think, sometimes, of where Uncle Sazi could be if he were not sick. What we are doing now he did ten years ago. He was loaded, Sipho, and the cars he drove were the flyest," Vusi said.

"At least he lived a little, he tasted things, drove the flyest," I said. "I cannot argue with that because he did live like a king for most of his life. It is the violence with which he is dying that I worry about. Sometimes he is like a person I never met before. He did live, though,

I can drink to that, at least. Let me check on the ladies."

The blunt changed lips. I hardly dragged four times and it was gone.

In the lounge, the girls danced to music while we watched muted soccer highlights. Within thirty minutes the trio were on couches, drowsy but pretending not to be. When Nana called, I realized I was the only one awake.

"I am ready. My father is home so don't park by the gate, I'll wait for you at the bus stop," she said.

"How much time before you reach the bus stop?"

"Ten minutes. I am going out the gate as we speak." I shook Vusi.

"Are you leaving?" he said.

"For sure. Where is the key for the Opel?"

He reached for his back pocket, handing me a single key. "Here. Don't switch off your phone—we may have to work later."

At the bus stop, Nana opened the door of the Opel with a wide smile. I followed suit, beaming toward her lips for a kiss.

"Surely you can tell me now. Where are we going?"

She settled in the passenger seat, fastening her seat belt. "Don't worry, baby, you will see," I said.

At the traffic lights at K Section, I remembered the debt I owed old man Mbatha. His house was visible from the main road. I made out two figures on the bench outside the White Room.

"Baby, detour first. There is something I forgot to do. I won't be long."

The two figures I could see from the main road had become one when I sat on the bench. I bought Nana a pint of orange juice from the tuck shop opposite old man Mbatha's house.

With old man Mbatha, there was no whistling. He was in simple garb—sandals, shorts and T-shirt—like someone you could meet in your neighborhood. That day, he was someone's father, brother, uncle, even lover. I placed R500 in front of him.

Old man Mbatha did not count it. Instead, he

threw the notes into a big bucket and took my head in his cold hands, saying, "Boy, go on, more doors will open soon."

On the way back to Nana in the Opel, I had planned the journey: a movie at the Gateway shopping mall, then a late lunch at a restaurant by the beach in Umhlanga Rocks. At least an hour parked by the sand in North Beach, just to ice the cake.

I ate up the freeway steadily, riding with my baby. I scrambled my brain in search of a tactful way to ask Nana what we had talked about the previous night. Mutterings of surprise. What had I said that made her smile so much? Had I apologized from inside a blur? The smile she wore on her face chased away my questions. I just looked into her eyes, mesmerized by her dimples and knowing smile.

"What's up? Why the smile?"

"Nothing. I'm happy because I'm rolling with you," she said.

It was as if she knew something about me I did not know she knew. I went with the flow—things seemed better anyway. Why mess up a good thing?

In the dazzle of the Gateway shopping mall, we went up lifts and escalators hand in hand. We checked at the cinemas first to get our times right. In the queue for movie tickets, I kept thinking of the "Sale" sign I had seen in the display window of the Hugo Boss shop. Nana chose the movie, a light romantic comedy appropriate for the mood. It was thirty minutes before the movie, so we chilled on couches in the cinema foyer. Her head was on my lap.

"At last, you watch a movie with me," she said.

"Other times I really don't have cash or I am busy

with fixing cars."

"Even if I have cash you don't want to come with me."

"I want to spend my own money, not your father's."

"When he has given it to me it becomes mine. Anyway, it is not about that; it is about me being with you. It is better now that you have a phone—we can talk all the time. Before, I'd call, missing you, and get mad if you were not there."

"Do you want anything from the snack kiosk?"

"Don't change the subject. Where were you, if not at home?"

Her playful accusatory finger pointed at me. Her face changed into a sulk. I laughed.

"I'm serious about that, Sipho, I don't want to hear stories about any girlfriends. I'm true to you, as you must be to me."

"You know it's only you," I said.

She smiled as if I had tickled her from inside.

"No chocolates—they give me pimples. No popcorn either. I did not come to the Gateway to floss. Buy me wine gums."

The lady at the entrance tore our tickets. We settled in before the forthcoming attractions trailers. They were fantastic, dynamic and fast. In the movie, everyone was clean. A blonde and a brunette fought for the affection of a guy. Nana snuggled under my arm on the armrest. She shifted her head onto my shoulder and assumed that position for the hour and a half the movie lasted. We laughed in unison in the darkness. The brunette won in the end.

At the Hugo Boss shop, I browsed through clothes while Nana sat on the sofa.

At the restaurant by the Umhlanga Rocks beach, Nana ate pasta. I wolfed down a medium/well-done rump steak. Outside the window, waves splashed on the rocks. Further away, two men kite-surfed gracefully.

"Look at them. That is us sixty years from now."

Nana pointed to an older couple on an afternoon walk along the beach.

She did not finish her meal, and asked the waiter to wrap it up.

In North Beach, we kissed in the back seat of the Opel. She let my hand roam all over her body, but held my wrist when I went too far.

"I am on my period, baby," she said.

I was content with smooches anyway. The aura of North Beach was pure calm. We chilled there for two hours. In front of us, waves carried and crashed surfers, cargo ships approached the harbor and the occasional fitness fiend jogged past.

"You can be sincere when you want to be. Your apology, and today—baby, you are lovely when you get like this. I wish the day were longer. My parents must stretch my curfew by an hour at least. I will be seventeen in less than a month, but I must stick to a curfew set when I was thirteen."

When I dropped her off, Nana gave me a deep, passionate kiss. "Text me later but make it long," she said.

"I'll try, baby, but I am not good with words."

"When you called yesterday you were very good. It is simple—you just say what you feel."

"I'll text but I will be waiting for yours, too," I said.

"Bye, baby, I had a wonderful time."

SIFISO MZOBE   89

I parked Vusi's Opel in the backyard at home and tried to relax in the empty house, but got bored quickly and called Musa.

"I heard you were on a date, Mr. Loverman. How did it go?" asked Musa.

"It was all right. Where are you?"

"Q Section. It is good you called, I want you to come with me to KwaMashu. I have been drinking all day; I need a driver. Are you busy?"

"No, Musa, I am bored. Come pick me up."

❖

My feelings about KwaMashu lie in a place that is not quite indifference and not exactly fear. The area is windy and dusty—at least, every time I went there during the day it was. A hit was pulled and I drove the getaway car. This added in no small way to my take on the place. Musa did not care, though. He picked me up in the same 325is. With him was a quiet, Versace-clad cat. It was the first time I met him, but it was through him that I got my first car.

It was also through this dresser-type cat that I understood that the township of KwaMashu was, and maybe still is, a faster criminal nation. What we did in other townships, they did faster and harder. He ran one of those houses you go to if you want to sell your stolen goods. All townships have these houses. In KwaMashu, though, there was such a house in every section.

I eventually came to know the dresser cat as Hugo. All he did for a living was connect buyers to sellers. Not only that, he was a master of accents: he spoke Indian English when Indians called, and went all colored when a caller from Wentworth rang. All white, too, when white club-owners wanted limited-edition cars. Hugo, the deceptively humble king of the black market—it was a plus to know him.

We stopped at one of those tuck shop/tavern/ payphone containers that have mushroomed all over the townships. What else but another Johnnie Walker Black? Sometimes I think liquor was the only point of our riding. We just had to refill, create some dream-like scenes and sins.

It was at the container that I bumped into a girl from my neighborhood. Her real name was Nompumelelo, but I called her Touchy—she always had to be feel-ing something and then let you know. I had kissed her once, and even then I bribed her with a chocolate bar she never received. That was in grade six.

It was cool between me and her, but the girls she rolled with—and Touchy was the ringleader in this— drank like Nicholas Cage in Leaving Las Vegas, only they did not die. She gave me the address of where she was, and mumbled something like, "Bring liquor; I'll organize you a chick."

All through my chatter with Touchy, Hugo was with two Mandrax addicts. From his conversation with the addicts, Hugo asked Musa if he knew anyone inter-ested in a dolphin-shaped BMW 328i.

"What color?" Musa said. "Green," replied one of the addicts.

Musa said he would find out, but in a detached, nonchalant way. A sort of maybe. Hugo told the ad-dicts to check him after an hour. Hugo was one of those people I just could never be. He always looked smart, forever dressed up. To chill at Hugo's, people had to dress up—I mean people from the same street, even. At his house I did see high-class chilling, though. The highest of high rollers dropped by, with girls fit for the Milan and Paris catwalks. Parked cars banged music. Girls chilled and looked pretty; others chilled, looked pretty and smoked; some chilled, looked pretty, smoked and drank. One girl rolled the longest-burning blunt I ever puffed. I went hard on the whiskey.

Call it a moment of clarity or plain drunken stupor, but I decided to buy the BMW that was up for sale. The addicts were back exactly on the hour, as per agreement. I gave Hugo R2 000. He paid the addicts R1 500, and they gave him R200 for helping them sell the car. In a minute Hugo made R700. All parties were satisfied. When I bought the car, I got a bit of attention from the girls, but it quickly died down as another high roller bought a chunk of gold chain also up for sale.

Musa led the way out of KwaMashu in the 325is; I followed in my new 328i. Before we left KwaMashu I picked up the chick that Touchy promised me. I didn't say much to her. I recall the complexion of her skin—a light peach bordering on yellow—but almost nothing else about her, except a white summer dress.

When we reached Umlazi, I hid the car at Vusi's. I knocked on his door in the backyard, but he was not there. I knew where he hid the keys, so I made myself at home.

I also remember that around 3:00 am I woke to take a piss. On my return to bed, my chick wanted a kiss. With the blue light of dawn on her yellow face, she looked like a ghost.

MORE DOORS OPEN

My eyes opened to a view of galvanized metal roof sheets. I heard raindrops exploding on contact with the roof. It was like the metal sheets were the last barrier to a flooding river that poured over Vusi's room.

A peach arm rested on my chest. Heavy, soft, warm. I swiftly peeled it away because my bladder also threatened a flood.

The toilet in Vusi's back room was bare of tiling and paintwork. Only a plastic curtain separated it from the bedroom. Wedged into the mix was a shower. I leaned on the hand basin and released my torrent into the toilet. I washed my hands and face in the basin, but found no mirror.

Plastered at the far end of the double bed was my ghost. She was on her stomach. Her bulbous ass made two mounds under the duvet. The sound of her breathing was almost a snore. She shifted to the center of the bed, arms spread wide.

A TV, DVD player and three-component music system sat on a stand in a corner. Recent car and soccer magazines were piled on the floor next to the stand. The ghost's white summer dress hung from the open door of the built-in wardrobe.

By the window I stepped on a torn condom wrapper. I lifted the curtain and saw water droplets scattered over the windowpane. When I opened the window, the rain felt light in the morning wind. From the sound on the roof sheets I had mistaken the sprinkle for a downpour. The room needed fresh air to dilute the heavy scent of whiskey breath, sex and cheap perfume.

My first car, the dolphin-shaped BMW 328i, was there all right—brute yet refined, a pure stunner covered in heavenly rainwater. I just needed to see it. My life had moved at a higher tempo since Musa's return from Joburg, and I needed to take a breather, a few minutes to make sure it was still me, to maybe pinch myself and ensure that it was not all a dream. I had dropped out of school, but was yet to decide what to do with my life. I fixed cars with Dad in our backyard, but it was a hand-to-mouth existence. Musa's plans promised money in large amounts; they also brought endless possibilities to my mind. It was my chance to build something. My chance to break the cycle of nothingness. To step into better things. When Musa put me in on the car scheme, I started to daydream of a future with children and a wife and a simple, straightforward business like owning taxis.

When I had time to project my thoughts—which was rare, with my ups and downs, liquor, weed and chicks—it became clear that outsiders could never understand the rules of criminal brotherhood. It was tricky; I mean, I was swimming toward the deep end of this pool, yet all the time I wondered if there were such things as rules. If you were Vusi, what would you do if you returned from a night in the city to find a stolen car you did not steal in your backyard and a drunken friend with his girl in your bed?

Through the window, I saw tiny Vusi circling the 328i. He opened the door and leaned back in the driver's seat. Both his hands grabbed the steering wheel. The bonnet shifted. He moved to open it, using a pocketknife fished from his back pocket. He left the bonnet, and turned what was left of the ignition with the knife. The engine started with a deep rumble. For some reason, he resisted the urge to rev it. Instead, he was back over the open bonnet, head nodding to the rumble in idle. He killed the engine and walked slowly toward me. I pulled up my pants and sat down on the edge of the bed.

"The green BMW is you?" Vusi said as he closed the door. He crossed the room to the plastic curtain.

"For sure," I said.

"Where did you get it?" he shouted over the flushing toilet.

"I bought it in KwaMashu. I was there with Musa and a friend of his."

"How much did you pay for it?"

He reappeared from behind the plastic curtain. "R2 000."

"You like to waste money. If only you told me you wanted this car. Here in Umlazi 328i's go for R1 500. It is a waste of money what you did. I must definitely teach you to steal so you will drive whatever you want, free of charge. It is fresh, though."

Vusi did not sweat it. He proceeded, pausing occasionally to check out the ass of my ghost, to tell me about a BMW 740i on the list that he had spotted in Umhlanga Ridge.

"This will be the easiest of them all. For one day

every week there's a complete hour when no one is watching it. It is your color too, Sipho—black."

"When are we getting it?" I said.

I followed his hand as a guide. We walked out the door to the sound of running water from behind the curtain. Vusi looked up at me with a smile laced with mischief.

"Where did you get her?" he said. "KwaMashu."

"You were wilding out there. Why did you not call me?"

"How could I? You were cozy with your trio. How did that pan out?"

"I had a blast. I just dropped them off."

Vusi's sister, Mimi, took some convincing when I asked her for a simple favor. My ghost wanted to leave—impatience was all over her face, emphasized by involuntary jerks of her right knee. Mimi was on her way to the city, already late.

"Please, Mimi, drop her off at the market or any other place where she can find transport," I pleaded.

"You and your friend Vusi can ruin a day. I asked him yesterday to lend me his car, explained exactly what time my appointment was. Now it is you and your stories. I don't understand how I fit into your mess."

"I am begging you, my sister. I am so tired that I cannot drive to the city. Please help me out."

"Okay, but make it quick. I am really late."

I met my ghost again, a few months later, in a dream so violent that the rain in it was blood. Her ass was still as firm, the rest of her a decade older.

My 328i was in Vusi's backyard. The rain made it look so desirable that a stupid idea darted across my mind: I seriously thought of taking it home. But the car was still hot, the engine number, paint color and tags still original. And it was broad daylight. I let the idea dart across until it disappeared.

A headache like a deep, loud gong battered me all the while. We were to move for the 740i later that afternoon. I declined Vusi's offer to take me home. He looked dumbfounded by my decision.

"It is really not a problem, Sipho. I can easily organize transport for you."

"Don't worry, I'll take a taxi. I want to ride out this headache," I said.

On purpose, I chose a taxi without music. I sat next to a heavily perfumed lady. Her attire told me she worked at the airport. I was heavily scented myself with alcohol and sweat. I toyed with the idea of starting a conversation with her, just for the sake of talking, but my resolve took over; I needed to clear my head.

I got home feeling dirty inside and out. I felt and smelled like it was two weeks since my last bath. When I got to the gap in the blue wall, I detected the aroma of frying bacon. It grew more distinct toward the kitchen.

Ma stood over the stove, over a frying pan full of pork strips. Nu sat at the kitchen table. Just like déjà vu—a memory out of the blue—a picture flashed into my mind from when I was about the same age as Nu, at the very table, next to the same stove. The same Carole King song filled the house. The same light on Nu's face as she smiled at everything Ma said. When I was child, I used to draw imaginary pictures of Ma's love for me. Under a silver sun, I played in the shade of the biggest shield in the world. Ma's love was the shield, with a shade so wide it covered places I never reached.

My sister Nu was infatuated with bubbles and mutton-curry pies. If she overheard that you were going to the city, she made sure to ask for her bubbles and pie. She saw me first and flung her arms wide. I remembered a promise made two weeks earlier.

"What do you have for me?" she said.

"I looked everywhere but all the stores were closed." I was taking chances.

Ever since she was a baby, Nu's face had adjusted quickly from happy to sad. It took only a split second for her to look at the floor and frown. Yet when she saw me, her smile was light but heavy with warmth. To disappoint Nu was to break my own heart. My hand fished out a R50 note from my pocket.

The pink note matched her pajamas. Her face altered just as quickly to happy. All the moment needed was a camera. She waved the note like a flag. I composed myself, methodically eliminating all clues of a hangover from my tongue. My mother despised liquor. Her back was to me.

"When did you get back?" I asked.

"Yesterday night, around eleven." Ma was concentrating on the frying pan. "How did you like being on your own?"

"It was boring because you were not here. The house was quiet, I was bored. Mostly all I did was sleep. I only went out as a favor to Musa. A friend of his who owns taxis was short of drivers, so I drove for him," I lied.

"You made some money for yourself; that is good. Where did you go?"

"Tongaat."

"Did you ask Musa about jobs in Joburg? You are too young to be a back-yard mechanic. There are things you still need to do, like finish school. These days, to get a job you must have matric at least."

"No, Ma, I did not ask him, but I will."

I moved to the lounge. It was good that the house smelled of bacon because it disguised the smell of alcohol on me. The steam from the bacon became my scent. Ma's attention remained on the pan.

It was all going according to my original plan: go home, greet and head straight for my room to sleep. I accomplished all my objectives—I got home, I greeted Ma, I went to sleep, but not in my room. "Not on my sofa, Sipho, you need to wash up and sleep," Ma shook me awake.

I went to my room, but I couldn't sleep. For two hours I was caught in that purgatory called half-sleep. I went from cars to houses to mountains to highways to airplanes to hearts to speech to love to hate to kill, but never to dying. I gave up. I woke up when I saw yellow flowers. Stupid half-sleep.

Hanging at the corner by Mama Mkhize's was the only other option. All my neighborhood friends were there. It was a long time since I had seen them. Nkulu and Ndumiso, flanked by the nut-job called Sticks, were sharing a quart of beer. A big talker, Sticks was the hero of all his stories. I took a few fives.

"How about a loose cigarette there, Sipho?" Sticks snatched the R5 coin I flipped in my hand.

"Buy two because I need to make a call with the change," I said. Sticks returned with five loose ciga-rettes and no change.

"How about watching the football genius Sticks do his thing today, Sipho?"

They all puffed on cigarettes. Sticks in particular enjoyed his. He tried unsuccessfully to blow smoke rings.

"I should dust off my boots and show you a thing or two, boys," I said.

I was good at soccer, but Sticks had the first touch they pay millions for in Europe. Sticks saw the gaps on a pitch and passed the ball there. As a soccer player, Sticks was blessed with the rare gift of making the play. He started moves and sometimes finished them off. His skills were better than Musa's and mine, but with a lesser engine. Sticks lacked stamina. He knew this and made sure his work on the pitch was done in the first half. In the second half he would just relax and spread the ball. I considered playing soccer with my neighborhood friends. I even imagined it: the dust, the plays, the exercise. Then Vusi called.

"Pick me up in ten minutes," he said.

I knew I was saying goodbye to my childhood, embracing manhood from a different angle. If there was a moment I could point to and say, this is when I left childhood behind, Vusi's phone call was that moment. It was the bridge. Before stolen cars, there was no substitute for soccer in my life. When the ball was at my feet, I was completely free. Soccer made sense to me. Unfortunately, in the township it rarely paid. Car theft was a better bet. I had the luxury of feeling sad for a minute, said a quick farewell to my dreams, spat on the tarmac and went home and changed. Vusi and the call to get the 740i—that second was the bridge. I chose money over freedom.

I changed into running shoes, track pants and a T-shirt. Ma was asleep. In the lounge, Dad and Nu were on separate planets. She was glued to the cartoons on TV, my father equally attached to his newspaper.

"What was wrong with the Opel?" Dad moved the paper.

"It needed brake pads and a service. I am taking it to the owner now," I said.

"You made some cash for yourself. That is good." The paper returned to its position in front of his face.

I found Vusi on the corner of the last turn to his house. He was sitting on the plastic cover of an electricity meter, dressed in trainers, track pants and T-shirt. In the car, he was withdrawn, pensive even. He was a veteran, yet it looked like he had doubts. I remained on edge until he spoke.

"R350 000 for a three-man share—would you do it?" he said. "What is the nature of the hustle?"

"Robbery. I am the lookout and getaway driver."

"If there are guns involved, I would not do it. They bring bad luck."

"I'm telling you, Sipho, if I go through with this one, maybe I can breathe a little. I'll even raise my game, be like Musa. No longer stealing but running things on a higher level."

"The way I look at it is that at the pace we are going now we will get to another level soon enough," I said.

"I hear you. But it is like insurance of sorts. What if the car scheme halts? That happens too; I see it all the time. It will be another way to distribute my eggs, not have them all in one basket. Slow down by the petrol garage; we'll sketch the plan there."

We were in Umhlanga Ridge. Our stop was a few houses from the target. Vusi bought sausage rolls and cooldrinks at the garage shop.

"They will gather soon. I'll drop you off a few houses down. You must relax, walk like you are a local boy. A lot of black people live here now. Be quick when you get to the 740i."

Vusi pulled out a metal rod with a perpendicular handle. Half the length was filed thin to resemble the tip of a flathead screwdriver.

"Stick this into the keyhole of the door. Add power when you turn it. Inside the car tear the padding around the ignition. Forget about wires. What you will be looking for is the base where all the wires converge. There is a coin-like metal plate there with two screws and a slash at the center. You stick this in the slash and turn it. The car should start. I don't need to tell you what to do when the car is on. You press the pedal to the metal. If you do all of this fast enough, we will be at Sibani's by the time they realize their car is gone."

I digested Vusi's instructions with a slow look at the reed forest on our right. The leaves rocked in the wind. The banks of reeds, silky green waves about half a kilometer wide, ran side by side with the freeway until both tapered into the horizon. In my chest, hooves of a thousand horses turned my heart into a drum on which they stomped out a beat.

"Be fast, Sipho. I'll turn around and park a few houses back. Check your mirrors when you get inside the car. I'll be there. I'll flash my lights if I see trouble, so make sure you check your mirrors."

As we waited for the 740i, I leaned back my seat

and thoroughly enjoyed the waves of the reed forest. Vusi was all over the place. Call after call on his phone. In and out of the garage shop for airtime recharge vouchers. All his conversations were outside the Opel, and conducted in whispers.

The first of the party to arrive was a bluish Benz with pre-registration papers on both windscreens. It quietly vanished through the open electric gate. All the other cars arrived to park on a strip of lawn outside a high wall. Ladies carried foil-covered trays from a minivan. A tinted bakkie. The 740i close behind.

The driver of the 740i took an eternity to get out, his hand clutching the edge of the rooftop as he slowly pulled the rest of his body. His step on the lush lawn was tentative, as if looking to find ground firm enough to step on. When he stood up, I could see he was tall, his shoulders bent and stiffened by the rigidities of age. The door of the 740i was barely closed when children spilled out of a station wagon to mob him. He nearly fell, but smiled and ran his hand through tiny mops of blonde and brunette hair. They all entered through the pedestrian gate. Vusi got into the Opel and dropped me next to the 740i.

The 740i was supposed to be a steal—pardon the pun. For one thing, it was unlocked. The party was at the back of the house; I smelt flamed meat and heard distant chatter. I opened the door of the car. Before even touching the ignition, I adjusted the rear-view mirror to place Vusi in the Opel at the center of my view. In the reflection, a cloud of cigarette smoke rose from the driver's window. I ripped out the padding around the ignition of the 740i, exposing the wires. I traced them back with my hand, all the way down the steering column. Threw a passing glance at the mirror—no flashing lights. At the base of the column I felt a metal plate with a slit and two screws. I checked the mirror to find the headlights of the Opel flashing. Hooves of a thousand horses thundered in unison. I looked in the mirror again; the lights were still flashing. I folded myself under the steering wheel.

I made out two female voices—loud at first, then drowned out. I peered through gaps in the steering wheel and saw two ladies in aprons picking up more trays from the open boot of the minivan in front. The calibrated stomp of hooves rang in my head. The women turned; I folded back into position under the steering wheel. Their voices were faint on approach, but rose in volume as they neared the 740i—only this time they did not pass. They were so close that I could hear exactly what they were saying.

"Goodness me! Uncle Robert left the headlights on again."

"He forgets all the time. I forget too; it comes with age. If we can forget, just imagine Uncle Robert..."

Their voices faded again. I lifted my head and saw them enter through the pedestrian gate.

I tried again, found the metal plate and rammed in Vusi's tool. The plate did not turn. When it did turn, none of the lights appeared that are supposed to flash when a car is on. I checked the mirror—no flashing lights from Vusi. I turned the metal plate; nothing happened. My attempts grew frantic. The lights that came on were the least desired—in the reflection, Vusi flashed anxiously. I skimmed up the seat. Through the gap made by an elevated headrest, I saw the tall frame of Uncle Robert laboring toward the driver's side. I jumped into the back seat. My hand synchronized with his hand. Uncle Robert slowly opened the driver's door while I opened mine behind the front passenger seat. He sat down with a thud I only half heard as I crept onto the lawn. Uncle Robert inspected the torn padding around the ignition.

In a second, I calculated the situation. In front of me, just across the road, was the reed forest. On my right, five houses away, Vusi was turning the Opel ready for a getaway. Behind me was Uncle Robert in the 740i, his head turned away from me to the open back door through which I had exited. I calculated the number of traffic lights we had passed on our way to Umhlanga, and in my mind saw police cars closing all possible exits as they hunted for a getaway car. Uncle Robert's hand clutched the edge of the car roof as he strained to get out. I knew how long the process took. I opted for the reed forest.

I took off my T-shirt and tied it over Vusi's tool and the wires for overriding the anti-hijack system. My feet ate up the forest. My lungs performed at maximum as I ran for my life. I hoped that my bare chest made me invisible in the reed forest, turned dark by dusky skies. I dared not look back. The reed fronds felt like razor blades on my torso, arms and face.

The reeds were shorter in the part of the forest nearest to the freeway. I bent over and took the last part on all fours. I took a breather when the freeway was a few steps away. I was far enough to afford a look back at Uncle Robert and the party. I strained my eyes, trying to focus on the fiasco I had left behind. I could not see Uncle Robert at first, but I soon saw blue lights flickering in the distance. Two police vans.

I slipped on my T-shirt, casting my eyes toward the low-cost housing across the freeway.

The unmistakable sound of a decelerating diesel engine shoved me back into the forest. Nine men with boyish frames descended from a bakkie. All were in grubby blue overalls.

"Six o'clock in the morning. I won't wait for anyone who is late," the driver said and drove off.

The men shouted and whistled at the accelerating bakkie. A few answered with vulgarities whispered in Zulu. I joined the gang and crossed the freeway into the neighborhood of low-cost houses.

The streets buzzed with evening bustle just like my township. I moved in darkness, avoiding the yellow glare of streetlights. At an empty communal tap, I washed dried blood from my face, neck and arms. I sat on the pavement under a dead light, desperate for a cigarette. I searched in the pockets of my track pants, but did not even find coins to buy a loose cigarette. My change must have dropped out in the reeds. My craving for a cigarette was soon replaced by a profound contentment: I did not get caught. I took refuge in that.

Thanks to luck and my ancestors, I still had my cellphone. I called Vusi.

"Where are you?" he barked.

"The low-cost houses across the freeway. I am next to a tuck shop with Cell C phones."

"Are you all right?"

"I'm all right. Just make sure you come with smokes. A cigarette headache is killing me."

"I'll be there now-now."

A chilly wind blew in the dark. My flesh throbbed

painfully where I had washed under the communal tap. The incisions made by the reeds were not deep but plentiful. Only my underarms were uncut.

Vusi parked in front of the tuck shop. He scanned the streets for me. I quickly got into the Opel. He lit two cigarettes.

"You think fast, Sipho. Most people would have chosen the getaway car. Don't worry about it; things like this happen. We'll try again somewhere else. Did the plate turn with the tool?"

He handed me a cigarette. "Yes, it turned with the tool."

"Your mistake; you must hold it still when you turn. It works like the key in the ignition. It is only the key that turns, not the whole thing," he said.

At the exit from the low-cost housing neighbor-hood, the arrows on a traffic board pointed at Phoenix to the left and Durban to the right. Vusi chose Phoenix.

❖

We scaled the steep hills of Phoenix. There was a BMW 735i at a shopping complex and a 750il outside a surgery. Neither was on the list.

"See what I was saying about breathing a little. If I had money, I would pay people to do this for me. All this driving around in the night, all this running." Vusi looked my way and feigned a smile.

Parked in a driveway in front of a closed gate was a silver BMW 740i. It was right in front of us.

"Here is a 740i. Stop," I said.

"They don't have reed forests here. If anything goes wrong, you run to me. There are many exits from Phoenix."

He dropped me next to the 740i.

I forced the tool into the keyhole of the driver's door, and turned it. All four doors unlocked. Inside, I ripped out the padding around the ignition to expose the wires. My hand immediately traced down to the metal plate. I held it firm, traced the slash, turned the tool. All the dials came to life. I put it in reverse, popped down the handbrake and slowly eased off the brake pedal. It rolled down the driveway. I shifted the gear lever into drive but did not touch the accelerator pedal. After turning into the next street, I switched on the headlights and pressed the accelerator to the floor.

Vusi followed in the Opel. On the freeway to Kloof he kept his distance, visible in the mirrors as a red dot that completely disappeared on bends.

"You are on your own after the Kloof off-ramp. I've decided to get this money, Sipho. I am tired of this running around, stealing every other day. When I come back, I will run things," he said over the phone.

"I hear you, my brother," I said.

"Slow down when you get to the suburbs. Prop up the back of your seat, strap on your seat belt. Drive it like it belongs to your father. I'll see you tomorrow for my cut. Good job, Sipho."

I reduced speed at the Kloof off-ramp. Vusi stayed on the freeway. With a single flash of his hazard lights, he vanished from view. I propped the back of my seat upright, strapped on my seat belt and drove the 740i well within the speed limit.

The 740i had impressive glide, handling and power. There was no anti-hijack system—lucky for me, because the override wires were lost in the reed forest, along with my coins and the remnants of my childhood. Later, when I got to Sibani's house, I made sure.

Outside Sibani's there was a white, limited-edition, six-speed, manual-transmission BMW 540i. The one Mdala wanted so much. Talk about road-huggers. It sat on black mag rims—just for the fuck of it.

I caught Sibani and Mdala off guard. They were drunk, their spirits free and high. They were entertaining a blond white guy in the games room. Rather, he was entertaining them, for he was loud and told all the stories. They called him Snow; at that time, he was the loudest white person I had ever met. His name was Snow because he sold blow.

"Hi, my name is Snow," he said.

"This is Sipho. He is the clocker of M5s I've been telling you about."

There was a lightness on Sibani's face. Not of skin complexion but of emotion. A genial smile ran across his face.

"Oh yes, I have heard about you, Mr. Clocker of Beasts. That is a talent, you know. I..."

Snow was hyper, and on some drug. Most sentences he started he did not finish, consumed by the white powder he made into three lines on a glass table and sniffed.

"What do you have for us today, Sipho?" Sibani said.

"I got a 740i, Sibani. It drives as if straight from the showroom." Sibani and Snow drank whiskey in its late teens. Mdala was a simple man—beer for him. No glass either—bottle to mouth. Sibani drank up the contents of his glass.

"I want to show you something." He led me to the garage.

"So you can see you don't jump over fences in vain."

His hand was on my shoulder. Although he was genuinely happy, with a jovial smile plastered on his face, there was a heaviness to Sibani's presence— a shade of darkness in his eyes, which remained emotionless.

In the garage there was a silver BMW 5 Series with tan leather seats.

"Transformation," Sibani said.

Instantly I knew what he was on about, for it was the 535i we had stolen at Amanzimtoti, the once-maroon glider.

"Snow bought it, so tonight we celebrate."

I did not ask the price. The 740i replaced the 535i in the garage. Snow drove off with erratic high revs.

An hour later, as three shots of Sibani's whiskey massaged my brain, R40 000 was laid in front of me.

"For a job well done, Sipho. You will get the money for the 7 Series tomorrow. I did not expect it so soon."

That was as far as he would go. Sibani was no talk-er. He was the prince of doers.

"No problem. Thank you, Sibani," I said.

I hitched a ride in Mdala's "new" 540i. A plas-tic bag on my lap held R40 000. Mdala was out of it and drove extra slow. He was talkative that night— alcohol liberates even the most conservative spirits. He mumbled all the way to Umlazi.

"Listen here, young blood, I have this scheme I run. I'll tell you this because I can see you are a go-getter.

Don't go wasting your money on girls at the clubs. I have this scheme I run, young blood, where R7 000 makes a profit of R14 000 in a matter of days. You tell me if you want in. In fact, you should want in. In this world, young blood, a man must distribute his eggs," Mdala said.

We parked by the blue wall.

"When can we start with your scheme, Mdala?" I said. "Soon, young blood. How is your father? Is he well?"

"He is all right, Mdala."

"Tell him I said 'salute.' Come see me tomorrow afternoon about the scheme, young blood, I'll tell you all about it."

In the kitchen I filled Ma's largest pot with water. I sat at the table in the dark, waiting for the water to boil. In the bathtub, the water turned a weak red from the blood on my torso. I shoved the plastic bag with money under my mattress. For close to an hour before I dozed off, I thought about calling Nana. Her voice was what I yearned for, not the words themselves. Sleep only came when I opted not to call. There was simply nothing to say.

NANA'S MATRIC DANCE

By 4:00 a.m. the following day, I was counting the money for the third time. It was R40 000 exactly. Not bad for a two man share. From my cut I reserved R7 000 for Mdala's scheme. Sleep did not come after that. I stared at the stained ceiling in my room until Dad, Ma and Nu woke.

Inspection in the mirror confirmed that my cuts were invisible to the passing eye but slightly defined to a roaming hand. I needed to avoid Ma and Dad just in case they woke with observant eyes. They might believe whatever lies I told about the cuts, but I did not want the questions. I made my bed and cleaned my room, mostly as a safeguard for my bank under the mattress. With my room clean, there was no reason for Ma to set foot inside. Better odds for my cash to remain undetected.

For the first time, I noticed how people under the same roof seldom look at each other. Nu headed to her cartoons on the television. She folded herself on the sofa in the lounge and watched, thumb in her mouth, eyes heavy with sleep. Ma trudged on behind her but remained on course to the kitchen.

My father's chirpy demeanor in the mornings was something that annoyed the whole family. He always woke with a springy step, while the rest of us took close to an hour to adjust. He remained effervescent till midday, his energy gradually lessening through the afternoon. By evening, he was usually so tired that he slept wherever he sat.

"Good to see you are busy so early. A man must wake up early, Sipho. I need your help with the gearbox of the Nissan three-liter outside. It has been fixed but you must help me fit it."

"No problem, Dad."

"I must buy parts for another car first. I'll be back around eleven. Get someone else to help you. I will pay." He exited through the kitchen door, enamel cup in hand.

Ma whipped up breakfast for Nu. The Jungle Oats came to the boil just as Ma placed a tray of her pies in the oven.

"Hi, Ma, how are you?" I said.

"All right. You woke up with so much energy. Why?"

"I've reached a point where I can no longer stand a dirty room."

"Tell your sister her food is ready."

Ma sat at the kitchen table to a generous bowl of Jungle Oats. "There is plenty left in the pot if you want some."

"I am all right for now, Ma. I want to go to the shops for airtime." There was an Avus-blue dolphin-shaped M3 outside Mama Mkhize's Tavern. I slid into Mama Mkhize's for a morning cigarette. The frame at the counter by the kitchen door looked familiar. It was Musa, with a can of soft drink and a packet of cigarettes. He beamed when he saw me.

"I was about to call. I was coming to see you. I only stopped here because of thirst," he said.

"I see. Vusi finally got you the M3 you wanted. I was with him yesterday, but he did not tell me anything."

"I so want to see Vusi. There is a rumor going around that he was rolling with the Cold Hearts. Something about a robbery in Stanger. When last did you see him?"

"Late yesterday. He did say something about a robbery and a three-man share."

"What is he thinking? I have warned him about those snakes. What is your story? What about the cash you were paid? Do you believe me now? I told you we will get this money."

I slapped the hand Musa held out, took his five.

"You did say it, Musa, I will not lie, but this much you did not specify. Actually, I wanted to buy clothes in the city. It is Nana's matric dance tomorrow and I must be fly."

"What happened to your face?"

"I ran through half a kilometer of reeds."

"You were lucky. I once ran through sugar cane. Now that will fuck you up."

"Reeds are not so bad. None of the cuts are deep."

"How much will you spend on clothes? There is a sale at the Hugo Boss shop."

"I can spend R5 000. I want a shirt, trousers and shoes."

"Why don't you buy a suit?"

"For a matric dance? No ways."

We stood by the side of the M3. I used Musa's wiry frame to block the view from my house while I smoked.

"So, are you ready to go? I don't know why you are hiding because your father can see you. Do you think he will assume that I am on fire, with these clouds of smoke coming from behind me? You might as well smoke in front of him."

Musa moved to the driver's side. Left out in the open, I kneeled by the passenger side and finished the rest of my cigarette.

"So what do you say? What time do you want to go?"

"Wait for me here. I'll be in and out. I'll just wash my face and get the cash. Please, Musa, don't turn at the ring; otherwise my father will see that I am leaving with you."

"All of a sudden it is wrong to roll with me?"

"No. He wants me to help him fit the gearbox of a four-by-four. Those things are so heavy that the last time I fitted one I took days to recover. I want to be fresh for Nana's dance."

Musa sank into the ivory leather seat of the M3. I left him smiling and shaking his head while I dashed home.

Ma and Nu were still adjusting to being awake. I was in and out. From my share, I counted a quick R5 000 and shoved the cash in my trouser pocket. I made a brisk dash for the bathroom to wash my face. Outside, my father's eyes were looking up toward Power.

❖

On the way to the city, Musa was easy on the accelerator of his M3. All he talked about were his two days in Tongaat.

"I was there with friends from Cape Town. It was crazy. Way too much whiskey, way too many girls. I think I'll lay off the whiskey for a few days. I forgot how sweet soft drinks tasted."

He sipped from his can. The swig seemed forced, unconvincing. "What was I saying?"

"Your friends from Cape Town…"

"Yes, my friends from Cape Town. I keep forgetting, maybe it is the ecstasy I popped, I just keep forgetting. Ecstasy—my friends from Cape Town, they push ecstasy. They told me they can get it for me at a reasonable price. They say it is big there. I am thinking we can move it here. Check out the thighs on that short skirt."

We were in the city. Musa's tale was cut off by the sight of a girl crossing the road at a red traffic light. He flashed the lights at her but she carried on without a glance at us.

At the Hugo Boss shop, I bought a shirt, formal trousers and brown suede shoes. At the door, I caught the side view of the M3 and found it was actually shaped like a dolphin.

"Did you really try it?" I said.

"Try what?"

"Ecstasy."

"I am on it as we speak. I tell you, Sipho, this is the best drug I ever tried."

He tossed me the car keys.

As we left the city, heading for his house, Musa waved at almost every girl we saw. When we hit the freeway, he raised the volume on the stereo and boosted the air conditioner.

"I am on it as we speak," he shouted over the stereo.

"How is it? I heard people say it makes you shit a lot."

"You must try it for yourself; forget what people say. Personally, I found that it took me on a peaceful journey of high. Wherever I was, it was all good. I mean, a car I hired there broke down on the freeway. We had to spend the whole night on the road but everyone was on ecstasy and the car had music. The following day everyone swore they had the time of their lives. You should see chicks when they are on it, Sipho; they dance as if walking through music."

I did not press hard on the M3. Nothing was out of the ordinary with Musa except the ferocity with which he chewed gum. When he looked right into my eyes, I was taken aback: it was like he was not there. His pupils constantly dilated and contracted.

"If we can bring it here—" Musa said in a deep voice laden with sincerity, "and, brother, it can be done—I am telling you, Sipho, we can change the city."

He bobbed his head to the music for a while but dozed off before we reached his house. I shook him awake.

"We are here already? You must stop driving so fast, Sipho," he said.

"I don't think I will try your ecstasy. If it can put you to sleep like this, imagine what it will make of me."

"I have not slept for two days," he said, opening the door.

I crushed from a stash of weed that was on the table in the lounge. Musa stretched out on the leather sofa.

"Will you smoke?"

"For sure," he said.

I rolled a quick blunt and moved to the balcony to launch it.

"But you have to put some cash in it, Sipho, if you want in on the ecstasy. A pack of one thousand pills is R14 000. If we sell the pills at R40 each, that is a profit of R26 000 to a pack," he shouted from the sofa. I nodded my head, partly in approval of the profit margin and partly from the buzz of the blunt.

"We will start it even—seven thousand, seven thousand—and it is just you and me on this one."

When schemes were laid out, it was quick and precise. "I'm in," I said.

"Make sure you have R7 000 by next Monday."

Musa rose from the sofa and came to the balcony when it was his turn to smoke the blunt. He dragged it once and passed it back.

"This weed is a booster for ecstasy. If I smoke, I will not sleep any more, which will mean three days without sleep," he said.

He was back on the sofa, asleep within a minute. I finished off the blunt on the balcony, in the quiet of the suburbs, to the music of trees.

In the lounge I flipped through channels, with the volume high to drown out Musa's snores. In the fridge there was orange juice, a tray of takeaway pasta and beers. I drank a beer dumpy in one gulp, but it tasted funny. It was the setting that was not right. Beer and weed were daily bread to us, but it just felt out of place in broad daylight. The combo went down well under the pitch black skies of night. I settled back on the sofa with a glass of cold water.

On television I caught a car program in the middle.

The boyish host thrashed the latest supercars around a racetrack with pure, childlike joy. He told the story of an older classic in an insert. A car with fine lines and chrome clambered up lush green hills. I pictured myself cruising over the same hills in a 1988 BMW M5—sunroof open, windows down.

A documentary about the effects of a drought on the wild animals of Central Africa started on the hour. A pride of lions ganged up on a resilient hippopotamus. She was no match for the cats, but she died on her own terms. She conjured a courageous escape from the cats, only to die of injuries from the attack in the mud of a scorched lake. My eyes grew heavy. I shook Musa awake. His eyes opened for a jiffy—wide red balls stretched to the maximum.

"I can't drive, take the is. The clothes you bought require a fly ride. If you see Vusi, tell him to call me."

Musa turned instantly to sleep. I picked up the stash of weed from the table. The Yale on Musa's front door locked behind me.

I looked for Vusi when I hit the township. His sister Mimi was on her cellphone at Vusi's gate in F Section.

"Hurry, I am on a call," she said.

"Is Vusi around?"

"When he left, he said he was going with you. Check him at Uncle Sazi's."

Mimi returned to her call. "You owe me," she shouted at me when I reversed. The thumb of her hand slid over the underside of her fingers. I pressed the accelerator and evaded paying for her favor.

Nana was in my room when I got home. My girlfriend was blessed with velvety dark brown skin. She was in front of the mirror in my room, under the glow of a naked light bulb, in a white dress. The dress was not just any kind of white, but a denser version of the color—like when a wave breaks. Her hair was pulled into a simple ponytail, which made her eyes slant upwards slightly when she looked at me.

"I was so worried, I thought you were not coming." Our faces kissed when we hugged.

The truth is, I thought the dance was a day later. She was lucky—as I was. I had the attire, a fair amount of cash and a car. I just went with the flow, acted like all was in my plans.

"I hope you are not wearing a suit because every boy there will be wearing one."

She went for the plastic bag with the clothes. "I'm not a suit person, nor am I a boy."

She was impressed by the clothes; her dimples appeared. I took a bath and chased Nu away from my room. We left to Ma's exaggerations about how good we looked.

Before we left the township, I checked Vusi again. He was not at his uncle's house. In F Section, it was Mimi who opened the kitchen door.

"He is not back yet, Sipho. Really, when last did you see him? Mama is worried now because he is not answering his phone," she said.

"Maybe it is a dead battery on his cellphone. Last time I saw him he was going to Stanger. Tell him to call me when..."

The horn of the 325is stopped me. Nana was pressing it.

"Go, Sipho, before Miss Beautiful over there hits you or something," Mimi said.

"Impatience, I tell you, Mimi, is perhaps her only

flaw."

In the car, Nana acted like she was mad at me, but I knew she only wanted attention.

"Who's she? One of your freaks?"

I did not answer. Instead I floored the 325is until she asked me to tone down and started talking sense —not that jealous, sulking nonsense.

The dance was at the Protea Hotel in Winkelspruit. It was easy to find because parked next door to the hotel was a Mercedes-Benz that Vusi had scouted. I bought a bottle of Johnnie Walker Black and some soda water at a bottle store near the hotel. We arrived to a rowdy reception. I had my qualms about the township upper class, but they went all out for the function. There was even a red carpet, confetti and fifteen cameramen.

Nana introduced me to her friends—pretty, friendly girls. The type of friendly often mistaken for flirty in the township. Food was served in three courses, of which the main course was the least tasty. I was hoping for a steak with maybe chips on the side. Instead, the plate dropped in front of me was almost empty, with something that was a slight variation of a pie (but had a French name) dead center. My mother's pies were tastier by a mile. I ate politely. Mostly I was mellowed out. Occasional trips to the 325is for a double Johnnie Walker Black and soda ensured that.

When music is slow, I can dance. My hand lay on the curve at the back of Nana's waist—my favorite part of her body. Four minutes of a song took my mind over, sideways and under. Perhaps it was the feeling that I floated in wonder—that's how it felt when she was in my hands. Her head rested on my chest. Four minutes of a song—the seconds made me forget and remember at once. Four minutes of a song absolved my dealings and stealing. Two hundred and forty seconds of a song—my heart pumped pure love.

I slithered away for a breather and a refill when the DJ played jumpy songs. On the balcony, I rolled a quick blunt and set it alight. Weed goes down well with whiskey. The sky was black. With me on the balcony was a group of five boys whose girlfriends were also alone on the dance floor. I revved up the blunt, downed more whiskey. Revved up again, downed more whiskey.

Two from the group on the balcony bummed my blunt. I gave them free rein over Musa's stash, which was, by the way, a dark green with orange whiskers. Let him who wants to smoke crush for himself. We connected into conversation as only drunk, high people do. It was just pointless chatter.

"Where are you from?"

"Umlazi."

"Really? I have relatives there. You know the shops in R Section?"

"Yes."

But the question that always cracked me up soon came from these suburban boys: "Do you know _____? He is a car thief, a friend of mine."

Names were trotted out. It amuses me how the better always want to connect. They want you to know that they also know.

The balcony got crowded when the girls came to check on us. I rolled a perfect blunt for the ladies, but passed on the ensuing rounds of smoking to concentrate on how to tell Nana what I was not sure she would approve of: ditching their after-party for Snow's party. My phone rang constantly; both Musa and Sibani pleading with me to join them at Snow's.

I did not sugar-coat it.

"We are not going to your after-party, but I'll take you to another party," I said.

"I don't mind as long as your party will be better than ours. If we ditch the after-party, it has to be for something better."

She sat on my lap in a chair in a corner of the balcony.

I don't know when in courtship the heart decides whether what you are going through is love. I did not know what love was, but in my head, as I envisioned my future, Nana was in every frame. In all the exotic cars I dreamed of, she had the passenger seat. In some of the cars she was the driver while I was in the passenger seat. Her presence in my future was that definite.

In the process of slow drinking, I was able to take in moments as snapshots and store them. We danced a bit more and finally ditched the party. I caught the time—it was exactly 23:55 on the car clock when we drove off. The Benz was parked next door; in a few days it would vanish.

I caught a mouthful of a gusty breeze and gulped it down when I rolled down the window. Nana's hand was glued to mine on the gear lever.

"You must teach me to drive. I may get a car when I go to tech next year," she said.

At Snow's we were the youngest couple there. It was the first time I saw Musa rolling with a sober girl. Being half drunk and captor of moments, I caught motivation and drive from Sibani when he handed me the money for the BMW 740i: R5 000 exactly. I counted it in the toilet when I urinated.

A fact about Snow: he lived in a dreamer's dream of a house in Ballito. I heard waves in every room. Where the majority of the people lounged, it was all about couches and sunken floors. Invincibility was in the air as we settled on a couch. I grabbed it. Another fact about Snow: he was the main mover of mind-distorters in KZN. His parties were rumored to offer—on the house, of course—strips of cocaine as thick as highway barrier lines. A rumor I proved to be fact.

In retrospect—hindsight being a motherfucker—the police should have caught us that day. With time, I have watched people grow tenfold who were then only small-time—the type of crews whose cases never come to trial. Snow's party was the only time ever that the multiracial faces of Durban crimeland were all under one roof. Most schemes still running today in Durban were put together that night at Snow's lounger heaven.

As a reminder of how small the world is, my neighbor Mama Mkhize was there. I caught her flirting eyes from our couch. We were on hard liquor—me and Musa—but sipped at extended intervals. Nana and Musa's chick nibbled on snacks, washed down with soft drinks.

Sibani, the boss of crimeland—the Original Gangsters saw raw genius in him—was in constant company with the veterans, the older crooks, the OGs. No doubt high-paying schemes floated back and forth. One after another they came and sat next to him. From our couch I saw he was bored, being polite.

He made an excuse, as if he was answering his phone, but came over to our couch instead. The lounge was filled with the who's who of Durban crimeland. They all waited in line for an audience with Sibani, but he came to our couch.

Maybe I caught too much, but the veterans' envy definitely came my way. I grabbed it.

"I'll steal them for a minute, ladies. Me and the boys have something to chew on," said Sibani, standing in front of our couch.

"You look bored out there," Musa said.

Sibani led us to a room with even longer and wider couches. The center of attraction was the main wall, which, bar one quarter, was covered by a white sheet. A movie projector zipped the ceiling.

"You don't want to be on top. They all come smiling at you. I'm tired and I'm fucking bored. I came here to enjoy the party, and these bastards tell me about strings to pull, the lamest fucking schemes. You remember I told you, Musa, when I was coming up, how none of them ever gave me the time of day. Now they come with their hands out and fake smiles. It is all bullshit when you are on top," Sibani said.

Talk about being on top. Sibani controlled all the schemes with the highest profits. If people wanted to make money in stolen cars, cloned credit cards, Snow's drugs, even telephone lines—it did not happen unless Sibani approved it. He was always paid.

Frustrated but icy cool, he passed a cigarette to Musa.

"We need the Benz soon. I already told the buyer to see me in two days. So you do what you do. Get the Benz so we can cross it off the list. Finish. Where is that partner of yours with the gold teeth?" Sibani said.

"He left for Stanger yesterday," I said.

"That is something else we need to discuss, Sibani," Musa said. I left them in a discussion of whispers.

I must have quickened my drinking intervals—an hour passed, and I caught nothing. I just lazed about on the couch with Nana. A joke here, some teasing there and countless kisses. Musa hardly talked to his chick. I never once saw him comfortable with a sober woman.

"You should see the front of this house, Sipho, it is beach sand," Nana said.

"It is true," Musa's chick assured me. "We went there while you were away with your friend."

"Baby, show me," I said.

I hooked Nana with my left arm, a glass of Glenfiddich in my right hand. The breeze sobered me a little—my captor instincts returned. I caught the huge scale of Snow's house. We rested a distance from the house.

Nana straddled me.

"I want you to build me a house like this one day," she said. "One day, baby, I will."

We kissed to the sound of the waves. She placed no boundaries to my roaming hands. I caught her surrender. A peppermint rolled from her tongue to mine.

We got a room when we returned to the house. Our lovemaking was neither unconstrained nor inhibited, just the right amount of mystery. Gentle at its zenith, the warmest of all sensations. Under the blue of dawn, Nana carved herself a new chamber in my heart. The first real love of my life.

I caught almost everything that day. Envy, drive,

surrender and—inevitably while we touched in the breeze—a slight fever.

WE BURY
A NATURAL

"Do you think they are too big?"

Nana was in the front of the full-length mirror that stood alone in the center of the wall. I had woken while she was in the shower. She shook her waist, then stood directly in my line of vision from the bed. Over the towel she had on, Nana grabbed chunks of flesh around her hips.

"No, baby, they give me something to hold on to. They help you move well when you are on top. Your hips give you power," I reassured her.

"They are too big. I must start working out soon. I won't even talk about my backside—that needs a professional training routine." Her towel fell. I watched her stride to the dressing table, naked. She broke the seal on a bottle of body lotion and poured some into her cupped hand. She stood at the edge of the bed, her foot balanced on the mattress while she applied body lotion to one leg and thigh. She shifted attention to the other leg with a stance that might have pulled a hamstring on many a man. Love and lust multiplied as I took in the contours of her naked body, unedited by clothes. She did the front of her torso while standing next to me.

"Please do my back."

"Come sit," I said, and shifted toward the center of the bed.

I applied the body lotion in as caressing a way as was humanly possible. Nana turned her head to me.

"I said apply the lotion, not foreplay," she said.

"I am doing as you said. I can't help it if I have magic hands."

She let out a sharp giggly laugh when my fingers touched the curve at the back of her waist. Her body jerked, then collapsed on top of mine, bumping onto the bulge between my legs. We kissed, but it did not go far.

"I have to get home," she said.

I pissed and washed my hands in the en suite bathroom. I picked up my clothes from the floor and got dressed. I looked out the window to gray skies. Waves broke on the beach with lingering spray.

The room Snow had given us looked like it had never been used. There were no pictures on the walls. The built-in wardrobe was devoid of clothes and hangers. The bathroom soap was fresh, with the logo not even slightly worn off. It was the same with the lotion—Nana was the one who broke the seal. The drawers of the dressing table were empty. The bed we slept in was of the highest quality, as was the timber of the wardrobe and dressing table. The room was just too neat—as if it had been built, painted, furnished and then locked.

Nana sat on the edge of the bed, her white dress on her lap.

"I won't iron it. It is not wrinkled at all."

I sat beside her, my hand wandering casually over her back. She held my wrist.

"I have to get home, baby. My parents gave me the night but not the whole morning, too. I must be back before nine at least so we will have more nights like this in the future."

She moved away. The bulge in my pants collapsed when she slithered into her dress and obliterated all odds of morning glory.

I made my way down the corridor to the empty lounge. Over the music system I heard voices behind a glass-and-aluminum sliding door. I peeled away the light curtain that flailed over it. The door opened to the pool area.

Smoke spewed from a brick braai stand in the corner. Musa's girl attended to the burning meat. Two other girls sat at the edge of the swimming pool, their feet in the water. Sibani, Musa and Snow sat on camping chairs next to the braai stand, huddled around a bottle of eighteen-year-old Glenfiddich whiskey.

Musa, the best holder of liquor I have ever known, was as sober as his chick. He rose from his seat to answer a call as I took fives from the guys.

"Sipho, did you hear me?"

Musa stood a distance from me. I lit a cigarette and poured soda water into a glass.

"Did you hear me, Sipho?"

I only caught the last part of what he said.

"...in a hijacked car. Back of his head blown out. I got the call just now."

"Who? What are you talking about, Musa?" I said.

"Vusi. Mimi called to say he is dead."

Musa sank into a camp chair, a scowl engraved on his face.

"I warned him about those snakes. If only you

heard Mimi on the phone. It was like the life in her was completely gone. She sounded hollow."

It was impossible to see Musa's eyes because he was wearing sunglasses. The harder I focused on the shades, the clearer was our reflection—Sibani, Snow and me, a portion of the pool, the dark green of the grass, the curtain at the sliding door. We looked straight at Musa. In the reflection, Sibani turned to me.

"Is it your friend with the gold teeth?"

"Yes, it is my friend with the gold teeth," I said.

Musa was up and about, restless. He called people who knew Vusi. I concentrated on the bubbles of soda water in my glass. I set my face to stone, my stare fixed on the effervescent water.

"I'm off, guys. I must go see Vusi's family. Just in case they need anything. Sibani, walk me out. We need to talk," Musa said.

I was left with Snow on the camping chairs. "He was a friend of yours, this guy who died?"

"I did not know him for that long a time, but he was a friend, yes. I was with him only the other day; it is hard to believe."

"What can you do about death? It comes when it comes. It takes away friends, mothers, brothers and sisters."

Snow picked up a CD cover from the grass next to his chair. Inside it was a tiny piece of plastic tied into a knot. He carefully untied the knot to reveal cocaine. He released the white powder onto the CD cover. From the side pocket of the camp chair he fished out a debit card and a R100 note. The card was instantly in use, dividing the powder into four white lines.

"Hold this for me," he said. The CD cover shifted to my hand. "Hold it still."

Snow rolled the note and used it to inhale three lines in one continuous go. I handed back the cover with the line that remained.

"The last one is yours," Snow said.

"I have never done blow."

I took the note.

"Do half the line for each side of your nose."

An instant brain scramble hit the center of my forehead, then spread like the tributaries of a river on a map. My lips, nose and tongue felt numb.

Snow wiped the remnants of the powder from the CD cover with his finger, then licked it. I lit a cigarette and watched the smoke rise and then disappear. Waves still bashed the beach. A ray of light pierced the gray blanket over the sky.

"Look at that light. With the waves moving it looks like a pen scribbling." Snow pointed to the ocean, then sipped from his glass. I looked at the single ray of light and thought of Vusi. He had taught me how to steal a car. He had put money into my pockets.

The day he left he had doubts. I remembered the day we told him about the plan. How he made all of us wait for sunrise.

The day I heard that Vusi was gone, the sun rose spectacularly to pierce the clouds with no intermediate stage between the pen of light and the total brightness that followed. I said a silent farewell to Vusi by a swimming pool in the morning glare at Ballito. I would be lying if I said I shed tears that morning, but my body cried. There was a burning knot in my throat, and the center of my chest was heavy from an invisible load, yet there was not a single tear. It was not like I was suppressing them, either. There were simply no tears to hold back. I just embraced the sun. See you when I see you, soldier, I said under my breath.

"Sipho!"

Nana was at the sliding door. She tapped at the face of her watch. On our way to the 325is, my step felt cushioned on air. Musa had left so suddenly he forgot about his chick. We were to drop her off in the city on our way to the township.

I bought red grape juice at a petrol station next to the flat where we dropped Musa's chick. A nasty backdrop of cocaine—from the top of my nasal cavity straight down the throat—called for a sweet wash-down. We drank the pint of juice with one straw. Nana's sips were more intense than mine, yet she wanted nothing when I asked her at the shops. The cocaine in me made everything move in slow motion.

"What is wrong?" Nana said.

"A friend of ours passed away."

"Sorry, baby. How did it happen?"

"We don't have details yet. I'll only know when I get to his house."

"Such bad news after a wonderful night. I did not know you had so many friends, but they are all older than you."

"I have always had older friends, since I was a child. But the one who passed away was my age."

"I'll call to check on you. You can come see me later; I think Ma is going to Pinetown, but I will call to let you know."

I watched her disappear through the gate at her house. With the world around me in slow motion,

Nana's step was frame by frame. Sticks and the gang were painting the house when I got home. A cousin of Sticks worked at a hardware in Isipingo and stole paint and sold it cheaply. He had found the weird blue paint for our wall. There was a long-standing agreement between him and my parents to provide paint for our house. Sticks and the gang somehow got a piece of the deal as painters. They said something, but I was tired and didn't have time to bullshit, so I did not answer. My family was not home. "Gone to city, chicken inside," said the note on the fridge.

I gave the chicken to the painting gang. "Wake me at twelve, Sticks," I said.

A sweating bottle of beer tilted to his open mouth. I moved closer and saw a crate of beers hidden behind paint containers. There was not enough strength in me to comment on the presence of alcohol while they worked. I was in no mood to hear Sticks's lies. What I needed was a few hours of sleep.

I woke up half an hour short of midday from a nightmare in which everyone I love died but I lived. I retrieved the cash from under the mattress and counted Vusi's share. It was R20 000, to which I added R2 000 from the preliminary sale of the BMW 740i we stole in Phoenix. Sibani had paid R5 000 for it, but I took the lion's share because I had done more. I gave Vusi less, not because he was dead but by law. Vusi had done the same for the 5 Series from Amanzimtoti. Even in death, principles applied. I shoved Vusi's cash into an envelope. From the window in my room I saw the tall frame of Musa come through the gap in the blue wall.

"The policeman I talked to said they found Vusi

dead in the same BMW driven by the Cold Hearts the day they were here."

I was with Musa in the backyard. He scraped a match on the blocks left over from the construction of the blue wall and lit up a blunt. His back was to the slopes of Power, his eyes cast to the bare ground of our backyard.

"They are testing me, Sipho. The Cold Hearts have no respect. They knew Vusi was my friend. They could have just double-crossed him; they did not have to kill him. See what I told you about the Cold Hearts? They kill for what they want."

"What exactly happened up there?"

"A herd boy discovered the car in a ditch by the road. When the police arrived, they ran the chassis number. They discovered that the car was hijacked in Durban. They ran Vusi's fingerprints with the Durban branch. He was on their records because he had a prior conviction for car theft. You will not believe this, but the officer who checked all this at the Durban branch lives in F Section. He is the one who told Vusi's mother. Without him I do not think we were ever going to find Vusi's body.

"I have to find the Cold Hearts. They must pay for this with their lives. It was not enough to kill Vusi; they tried to hide his body, too. The same car was used in a cigarette wholesale robbery earlier. Eyewitnesses to the robbery said there were three men. The owner of the wholesale claimed the robbers made off with R350 000. Yet only Vusi was found in the car. He was shot so many times his mother had to identify his body by birthmarks and gold teeth. From the number of gunshot wounds to his head I think we will say our goodbyes to a closed casket."

Musa passed the blunt.

"It is a cruel way to go—in violence and alone."

"It goes without saying, my friend, that the Cold Hearts have signed their death warrants. Sibani and I will see to that."

"They do not deserve to live," I said.

"If there is any cash of Vusi's with you, please take it to his mother. I am off to the city—Mimi wants quotations from funeral homes. I'll check you later."

"Later, Musa."

Shock reverberated over crimeland, and there was genuine sadness on our part because in Vusi we had lost a natural. He died in a way that everyone dreads—in violence and alone, shot through the head. The streets were talking, and the words took the form of a question: Why did he scheme with the Cold Hearts? Look at it this way, I still say: R350 000, split three ways. We all play a game of chance.

The Cold Hearts simply disappeared. Informers claimed to see them everywhere—in Cape Town, skipping the country, six feet under, living lavish in the rural Eastern Cape, none of which was true.

❖

I stalled for as long as possible, then took a long bath. My hands and feet shriveled from staying in the water too long, although I was in the bath for only thirty minutes. At the car wash, I hardly smoked five cigarettes and the 325is was gleaming. My weed merchant was not home. I had no excuse—no thumb to hide behind—so I made my way to Vusi's house.

My timing was terrible. Mimi was in the kitchen.

"I heard about it. I am so sorry, my sister," I said.

She just looked at me, the whites of her eyes a faint ruby from crying too long.

"I have this thing of Vusi's." I showed her the envelope.

"If it is money, you need to see Ma," she said.

Portrait of a grieving mother blanketed on a mattress on the floor and a solitary, slow-burning candle. She sat so that her upper body rested on her left hand for balance. Her eyes were hidden from me; she looked at the floor the whole time. I guessed that the whites of her eyes were probably maroon, for Vusi was once inside her. I kneeled down.

"I'm sorry for your loss, Ma. I just want to say it is not only you who lost but all of us as Vusi's friends. Here is something of his I was supposed to give him today."

I handed over the envelope. "Thank you, my boy."

Her words were slow, almost muted.

In my short life I had been to a handful of wakes and houses in grief. We'd hang around at the back of the house, ready to do whatever was asked of us. At my age, to be actually in a room with the grieving mother was rare. That day I understood why. It was an unyielding, heavy moment. Vusi's mother sat in front of me, defeated.

I wanted to say something, to bridge the space between us, but found no words.

Mimi gave me so much to do that I spent the whole afternoon there. I fetched relatives from the city, moved furniture out of the way, even went to the shops for groceries. All these chores set me up for a second encounter with Vusi's mother.

People who come around to convey condolences come mostly in the morning, at midday and at night. In the afternoon the grieving family is free in a way. I was about to leave. In fact, I was waiting for Mimi by the kitchen door to tell her I was going. Vusi's mother was outside getting some air and light. Yes, I was right, the whites of her eyes were a blood red. She took my hand as we moved around the house to rest on a bench near my BMW 328i, which was still parked in their backyard.

"Mimi says the car is yours. You have to move it before the nosy relatives arrive. Where do you stay?" Her voice was slightly stronger.

"M Section."

"Your surname?"

"Khumalo."

"And your parents, what do they do?"

"My mother works at Clairwood Hospital; my father is a mechanic."

"At home, how many are you?"

"I have a sister who is ten, and me."

"Our boys and this money..." She looked at me with pleading red eyes, her voice soft like when a parent reveals a secret.

"We know it is hard for you but this is no way to live. Parents should not bury their children—it is the other way round. Money may rule everything, but it is not the beginning and end. It is because of this money that my boy perished and the details are vague."

"I hear you, Ma. I will pick up the car before the sun sets," I said. It was hardly preaching, but in her way Vusi's mother tried to reach me. In my mind rang questions without answers. Are we born just to chase after cash and then die? Out of the gate, I pictured an opposite scenario where Vusi did not steal cars. Where he dropped out of school but decided not to hustle. Always at home asking his unemployed mother for cash. Which was better? I considered the paradox as I started the 325is. Simultaneously with the rumble of the engine, the screen on my cellphone lit up. A text message from Nana: "Just woke up. Ma did not leave after all. Miss u. Thanx 4 last night. Call l8r or send SMS. Luv u."

❖

I went to J Section and picked up Mdala, who was on his phone the whole time until we got to Vusi's house in F Section, in peak-hour traffic. Mdala had been roped in for a cameo appearance in our car scheme. The show had to go on. We were to get the Benz later that night. I also needed him to shepherd me out of the township, and afternoon peak hour is the best time to move a hot car. There was space in the garage at Musa's house for my 328i.

Mdala's brand of escorting was new to me. He kept me three cars behind him.

"Don't answer any other call except mine until we get to Musa's," Mdala said when we left Vusi's, but he did not call me even once.

At Musa's we waited for the darkness with an intense session of weed smoking. I dozed off on the sofa.

"You don't sleep, young blood. Sleep is important. The body needs to rest..." were the last words I heard before falling into a warm, dreamless nap.

My eyes opened to the National Geographic channel on the television. On the balcony, Mdala and Musa were sharing a blunt in silence. On screen, cranes and tugboats were depositing boulders into coastal waters somewhere.

"At last you are awake, young blood. Check what the Arabs are building. Reclaiming land from the sea. It captures the imagination, young blood."

Boulders piled up to form a structure that, from the air, was shaped like a palm tree. Sand was pumped to layer over the boulders. After numerous stages of compacting, houses mushroomed on the structure. The trunk of the palm tree was the connection of the structure to the mainland.

"Wash that face so we can leave. I don't want you sleeping on me, young blood," Mdala said.

I splashed water over my face in the bathroom down the corridor. In the mirror, my eyes were open but the rest of my face was still asleep. The only time I felt fresh was on the freeway. We drove to Winkelspruit in Musa's M3. Mdala opened the passenger seat window; gusts of an awakening breeze nudged a volt of focus into me in the back seat. In the driver's seat, Musa barked out our attack formation.

"Vusi told me the Mercedes-Benz arrives every night at nine without fail. The owner parks it in the driveway. After about thirty minutes he will leave to fetch his daughter; then he returns around twelve, but that time he will open the gate and park the car inside. The only time we can get it is in the thirty minutes when it is parked in the driveway from the first time he arrives. There is plenty of darkness in the trees opposite the house. I will leave you there."

Mdala nodded. Musa stepped on the accelerator.

He dropped us three houses from the target, but waited at a takeaway near the exit road. In darkness, we took our positions behind the trees opposite the house.

We did not wait long for the Mercedes-Benz. A few minutes after nine, it tilted up the soft incline of the driveway. The owner did not switch it off and used the pedestrian gate. He left the engine running to open the main gate. A change of plan.

I searched for Mdala's eyes in the darkness. I wanted to know, what next? Mdala was nowhere to be seen. I located his hunched shape across the road. His swift feet belied his age. Mdala was at the gate with a nine-millimeter pistol cocked to the back of the man's head. I followed close behind. Mdala dragged him to the passenger seat of the car. He pressed his knee on the man's back. I slipped into the driver's seat.

"Anti-hijack, where is it?" Mdala whispered to the man. "Below the steering wheel," he whispered back.

I pinpointed a small knob under the steering wheel. Mdala turned his gun to hold it by the barrel, and used the butt on the back of the man's head. Mdala threw him out of the car. My thumb was ready to pop the handbrake down, the car already in reverse.

The headlights were on the man as I rolled the car down the driveway. The damage from the pistol-whipping was evident—a red line snaked from the back of his head down his light blue shirt. He stumbled to the gate but fell in a heap.

We were out of there quickly. Musa followed five minutes after we made our exit. He caught up with us at his house. I parked the Mercedes-Benz in Musa's garage, next to my dolphin-shaped 328i. In the lounge, Musa handed Mdala R5 000.

"You can shove a car, young blood." Mdala gave me my share—R2 500.

"He should be a racing driver, this one. Do you want to check out the city? There are varsity chicks waiting for me in Morningside," Musa said.

"I am drowsy, guys, I need sleep. And I think I caught a cold at Snow's," I said.

"I am game," Mdala said.

❖

We were to chill until after Vusi's funeral, or rather that was the plan. In the following days, I gave Musa the cash for the ecstasy game. He was at his house drinking with two drunk chicks.

"The pills will arrive in five days. In the morning I clocked the M3. I can organize you a chick if you want."

He was talkative and excitable. "Where is Mdala?" I said.

"He left in the morning. Check him at his house, because when he left, he said he wanted to sleep," Musa said.

I did not stay long, for I was curious about Mdala's scheme, the one that bubbled under when he was drunk. I was doing my best, trying to be a man— making plans, plotting.

Mdala was with his wife, and they were drinking, of all things, tea. His wife was in a silk dress. When she excused herself from the lounge, bright red roses on white silk exited the room. Mdala offered me a cup of tea, which I declined. For business, we moved to an outside room that reeked of weed smoke. Mdala had a stash of genuine Swazi marijuana—the Dom Pérignon of weed. It felt like velvet in my hands when I crushed it, and like electricity to the lungs when I lit the blunt.

"Mandrax is a game of 200% profits, but if you sell it to wholesalers, young blood, they buy it at R21 a pill. I get it at R7 a pill. You are fast on the steering wheel and you can roll a perfect blunt. I can put you in for free but you have to return the R7. You don't need money to start, but I will put you in through my name so do not fuck it up."

"I won't fuck it up, Mdala."

I passed the blunt to his waiting hand.

"I am serious, young blood, this is money for a lifetime. I will organize, then give you a call next week. In the meantime make connections, because pills will stress you if you cannot move them fast." Mdala made light work of the blunt, turning it to ash with hurried drags.

❖

"Is this Sipho?"

"Yes."

"Can you pick us up at eight?"

The voice at the other end of my cellphone was hollow, splintered and unrecognizable.

"Who am I speaking to?"

"Sazi, Vusi's uncle. Can you pick us up at eight? We need to dress Vusi's body for the wake."

He let out a labored cough.

"No problem, Uncle Sazi, I will be there at eight," I said.

It was early, around five in the morning, but I did not go back to sleep. A quick count of the cash under my mattress showed R22 500. I succumbed to the craving for a morning cigarette and tiptoed to the kitchen door for a puff in the backyard. I sat on the leftover blocks. The persistent darkness of a wintry dawn hung in the air, the stars clear and bright like it was midnight.

A light came on in the kitchen. It was my father with his enamel cup. He sat at the table waiting for the water in the kettle to boil. I hurried the cigarette. When he opened the door, I was laying out our working mat under the Nissan four-by-four.

"You woke up early. How are you?"

"I am all right, Dad. I just remembered we had this gearbox job to do."

"It is good if you still remember. For a while there I thought I'd lost you to the streets."

"There is no such thing, Dad. I have just been busy, that's all. Musa knows a lot of people with car problems."

"The water is still hot—pour a cup of coffee."

"I am fine, Dad. Don't worry."

"We cannot fit the gearbox yet. The engineers fucked it up. I am taking it back today."

He sat on the blocks, steaming cup in hand, his gaze fixed on the slopes of Power.

"It looks like this winter will be a cold one," I said, trying to break the silence.

"For us who work in the open, I just hope it is as stubborn as summer was. Work is more productive in lower temperatures. How is your friend Musa?"

"He is doing well, Dad. He has a house in Westville

now and two BMWs."

"Make that one BMW, because the 325is is always with you."

"Well, you know Musa. He has always been a good friend."

"How is it on petrol?"

"Heavy. But the problem is with the engine."

"What is wrong with the engine?"

"It just keeps begging for acceleration."

"And there goes your petrol."

"You know the story, Dad."

"Does he ever visit them? His aunt, I mean. Does Musa ever visit them?" Dad asked, pointing toward Power.

"I can't say. It is not a subject that has come up, but I will ask him."

My father stretched his arms, then gulped down the remains of the coffee.

"I am going to sleep a bit. The gearbox people only open at nine."

"I'll take a bath and be off. My appointment is at eight."

"Try to tune the channels. Especially the one with the cartoons. Your sister was complaining about the quality of the picture."

He went inside through the kitchen door. Prickly stabs of the morning chill on my face and arms drove me into the house as well. I parked at Vusi's around eight. His uncle Sazi was sitting on a plastic chair by the gate. At his side, a man of sturdy build towered over him. A gym bag strapped over his shoulder looked tiny on his massive frame. He helped Sazi up when I switched off the engine.

I did not need to have known Sazi in his prime to realize he was in bad health. He was only skin and bone, as if the flesh in between had dissolved. They trudged toward the car.

"Better he sits in the front seat so it will be easier when I want to lift him up." The voice from the giant was deep and polite, with a strong Port Shepstone accent.

Sazi covered only a quarter of the front seat. I popped down the back of my seat. The tall frame disappeared into the back.

"You see, I told you Vusi had many friends."

Sazi turned to the back seat. His voice was labored, shattered, fading at the end. Sazi struggled for breath all the way to the funeral home. His directions were an effort—he came close to hyperventilation every time he said "left" or "right."

"We are here, nephew. We have come to take you home," Sazi said when we arrived.

We were in the city. Sincere affection laced Sazi's words. He spoke as if Vusi were alive and next to him. I killed the engine of the 325is. Sazi pulled hard on the door handle. He pushed the door but it barely opened. The attempt took a lot out of him; his breath grew heavy and rapid.

"Don't waste your strength, Sazi. I will open the door for you," said the giant in the back seat.

I followed them to a glass door below a sign with the words "Nzama Funeral Home." At the reception desk, a prematurely gray-haired, blank-faced man attended to us. Sazi signed a form. The man led us to a chilly room with silver drawers lining the walls.

"Vusi Shange, closed casket?"

His hand was on the handle of a drawer at waist height. Sazi concurred with a nod. The drawer rolled out.

Vusi's body rested on a metal tray. The head was extensively bandaged, the rest of the body pale and naked. Sazi reached out for Vusi's hand, examined it intently and turned to the giant.

"It is him."

Sazi let out a quiet sob. He fell to the floor, with tears on his cheeks. The giant was quick to pick him up.

"Can we have a moment alone?" Sazi's words were barely audible.

"Certainly. Just tell me when you are through. I will be at reception," said the blank-faced man. He exited the room.

"You are also free to go, Sipho. We will return home in the hearse. The things we are about to do require only family members."

Sazi's face regained some composure but his eyes showered uncontrollable tears.

The gym bag contained Vusi's clothes. The giant laid out a T-shirt, jeans, belt and shoes—all Hugo Boss—on a table in the center of the room. I heard the sound of metal on metal when I left. When I looked back, two hunting knives were being handed to Sazi. Sazi placed the knives in Vusi's lifeless hands and pressed the stiff fingers around the handles. He placed his hand on Vusi's chest. Sazi's eyes met mine, and I hurried my step to the door.

"As they killed you, my nephew, so we arm you to kill them. As they spilled your blood, use these knives and gouge out..." I heard him say to Vusi's body as I closed the door.

At the beach, I washed my hands and face with sea water. I opened both windows and the sunroof. The sound of crashing waves seemed louder with the stereo off. In all the thoughts that raced in my head, Vusi was prominent—bandage over his head, armed with two knives in a closed casket. In my mind, it was Ma grieving over a closed casket. Musa promising to kill those who had killed me. My father arming me with knives. My sister Nu crying for me. I leaned my seat back and cried.

I checked the time and concluded that Nana was in the middle of a class in school because I only got voicemail on her phone. On the way back to the township I bought a bottle of Johnnie Walker Black for consumption at the wake.

I phoned my uncle Stan for a meeting on the Monday after Vusi's funeral. Family and business do not mix, they say, but I needed pointers on the drug game. And Uncle Stan was the genuine item.

He had made a diamond life for himself by selling instruments to forget.

❖

On the evening of the wake, Musa picked me up in the M3. He bought apple juice, water and ice at Mama Mkhize's. We arrived at Vusi's house to the sound of church songs bellowing from the tent in the front yard. We saw Mimi for maybe five minutes. Our modus operandi for the night was to down the whiskey in Musa's car.

Deep into the night—our liquor finished, women praying and singing with occasional wailing—we left to buy another bottle of Johnnie Walker Black.

"There is one thing I did not do for Vusi." We were on the freeway to Montclair.

"What is it, Musa?"

"I did not get Vusi the car he loved; none of the orders came through for me. It will be a crime if I don't get it. It'd be plain wrong."

"What car are you talking about?"

"You don't know?"

"Know what?"

"When a car thief dies, we must steal a car that he loved and burn it at his funeral."

"What car did Vusi love?"

"Golf VR6."

Musa withdrew cash at an ATM in Montclair. We shared a cigarette on the pavement, as he was fussy about smoking in the M3.

"Jacobs or Lamontville, which one is nearer?" Musa said.

"Lamontville is on our way."

"Do you think they have Johnnie Walker Black there?"

"I don't know. Let us try Jacobs first. I'll drive if you are tired." I passed him the cigarette.

"No speeding today, Sipho."

He tossed me the key. I adjusted the driver's seat and started the car. On the pavement Musa answered a call. I fiddled with the stereo. A car parked behind us. Musa opened the passenger door and got in. The car behind us switched off its lights. I made out the sign on the front grille; next to the VW logo was a shiny VR6 badge.

"Here is a VR6, Musa."

"Where?"

Musa searched the side mirror. "Right behind us."

"Is it a Golf?"

"No, it is a Jetta. Green."

The driver's door of the Jetta opened. A boyish-looking Indian man rushed to the ATM.

"I am taking it," Musa said.

The Indian man rushed back. The hazard lights blinked when he pressed the immobilizer.

"We will meet up at my house." Musa crept out of the M3.

In the rear-view mirror, I saw Musa's wiry frame rise to point a pistol at the man's head. The car keys and cellphone were passed to Musa's free hand.

"Run! If you look back, I'll fucking shoot you!" Musa barked at the man, who took off at a great pace, almost falling as he rounded a corner.

We raced up to Westville. Musa gave the VR6 his best. I was right on his tail and shoved his M3 through the corners.

We placed a car cover over the VR6 under a carport in Musa's backyard.

❖

At the funeral, as Vusi's casket was lowered to rest six feet under, we spun the Jetta VR6. When the procession left the cemetery for lunch at Vusi's house, we stayed behind and burned the car. Musa threw a Molotov cocktail into the cabin. The leather seats ate the flames with vigor. The upholstery churned out acrid black smoke at the tip of a scarlet flame. White smoke from the bonnet turned black. The paintwork on the VR6 melted from green to black to ashy gray in minutes.

"It will explode now. We can watch from my car," Musa said.

We moved to the M3. While my eyes were arrested by the flaming VR6, Musa was the picture of indifference. He did not even look at the burning car. He conducted a lethargic search through his CD holder. He turned to me, a pinch of exasperation on his face.

"The disc I am looking for is in Sibani's car," he said.

He started the M3 and shifted it into first gear. I rolled down the window on my side, stuck on the magnificence of the orange flames. The explosion of the petrol tank was actually white in color and powerful enough to lift the back of the VR6 almost a meter into the air. Balls of black smoke soared into the sky. The flames turned back to orange as we drove off. We did not go back to Vusi's house.

At a mall on the outskirts of the township Musa bought a case of Johnnie Walker Black.

"So much whiskey, Musa. Are you having a party?"

"This is for Vusi's after-tears party. We have cried for him at his funeral. Tonight, we wipe away the tears and celebrate his life."

"Where is this party?"

"Westville, my house."

I looked back at the township as we joined the freeway to Westville. The great balls of black smoke from the cemetery looked minute in the distance, like a black string dangling from the heavens.

"Musa?" I said.

"Yes, my brother."

His eyes were stuck on the road.

"Burn a white dolphin-shaped M5 for me when I die."

"If I am still alive I will, my brother."

He turned up the volume on the stereo.

TAR RAiN

On the freeway to Musa's house in Westville, ours was a ride in contemplative silence. "Thank you, my brother" were the only words to come from my mouth when Musa passed on a cigarette. Each of us was alone with our thoughts. Musa's step on the accelerator pedal was smooth, and I could feel myself falling asleep. My eyes closed, and my head filled with rapidly changing images that quickly went out of focus. Soon, they turned into a blinding blur that crumbled into specks of black.

My eyes opened when Musa killed the engine. My first thought was of the BMW 328i inside the garage in front of us. Musa parked just as I was at the opening shot of a dream: in a landscape of blue clouds I stood in front of a silver garage door, car keys and remote control in hand. I pressed the remote control but woke as the silver door tilted up. As my eyes opened, it all crumbled down; the indigo lighting was replaced by yellowish silver. With the M3 switched off, I felt the piercing stab of the winter sun.

"How far are your guys with my 328i?" I asked.

"The only thing outstanding is the paintwork. The painter is coming tomorrow."

Musa picked up the case of whiskey from the boot

of the M3, with a feeble attempt at urgency.

"I invited my crew of girls from Tongaat. They all work, Sipho. From now on, I will date chicks who work. They buy their own booze and they drive. You'll see, we will vibe with them the whole night without spending a cent."

"Are they pretty?"

I opened the door to his house. "You will decide," Musa said.

We stretched out in camping chairs on the balcony. Between us was a bottle of whiskey, two glasses, still mineral water, apple juice and ice cubes.

"I have weed if you want it."

Musa twisted the cap off the whiskey bottle. "Maybe later, Musa," I said.

Neither of us bothered to turn on the TV or music. We sat in the camping chairs, the sound of trees swaying in the wind the only soundtrack to the silence.

"You will supervise the painters, Sipho, because I will be in Tongaat tomorrow. I have two appointments there," Musa said, breaking the silence.

The time we spent at Vusi's wake told, for we soon dozed off. Musa was the first to fall; he snored after just one sip from his glass. I leaned back and tried to replay the dream. What was beyond the silver door? Maybe a supercar stuck to the garage floor, or Nana and two children, with her face in a house of light that floated on indigo clouds. I saw manicured lawns lush and green as my backyard. What I got for my troubles was the blankness of sleep.

The bell of the intercom shook us awake. "They are here."

"Who's here?"

"My crew from Tongaat."

Musa wiped sleep from his eyes. With a lively spring, he leapt for the intercom.

My stare locked on my elongated afternoon shadow. I picked myself up. The ice cubes in my glass were smooth and brittle, almost completely melted in the whiskey, water and apple juice mix.

In the bathroom, I splashed my face with water. When I am tired, fatigue manifests as a heavy load unevenly shared over the shoulder blades. In the mirror, my left shoulder slouched noticeably. I stretched out my arms in an attempt to shed the load. Through the gap in the open bathroom window, I saw a convoy of four hatchbacks come through the gate.

Twelve girls off-loaded four cooler boxes. Musa swam in an ocean of hugs, his wiry frame engulfed in arms and thick, shapely bodies. All the girls were in jeans—it was curves galore.

The Tongaat crew scattered over the lounge and balcony. I quickly surveyed their faces and concluded they were all older than us, their bodies slightly plumped by age—like the women in Renaissance paintings, but black.

The faint aroma of weed that always lingered in Musa's house mingled with flowery perfume as the girls crisscrossed the lounge. Their cooler boxes were placed on the balcony, directed there by a girl with a boastful gait who was hand in hand with Musa. Ample space and the large sofas in the lounge meant all the girls could sit in comfort. Many of them were clutching ciders. On the balcony, two voluptuous figures sat on the cooler boxes. One smoked a cigarette while the other read the story on the back of the whiskey bottle. The bass from the speakers filled the fragrant lounge. Vusi's aftertears party was in full swing.

I was not drunk enough to socialize with the girls, so I hid away in the kitchen. In the fridge there was some leftover takeaway chicken. I pulled up a chair and devoured a drumstick.

"Where is the meat? We were at a wedding where they did not feed us."

A girl who looked like she was the oldest in the clique stood over me, a flash of gold between her front teeth.

"In the fridge, but it needs spices," I said.

"Show me where they are. I'll spice the meat. What is your name?"

"Sipho."

"I am Zandile; do you live around here too?"

"No, M Section in Umlazi."

"What about those spices? Will you braai the meat for us? I am so hungry I will collapse any moment now."

In a cupboard above the fridge, the spices were in a container marked Sugar.

"Bring the meat outside when you are done spicing. I will start the fire. Where do you live, Zandile?"

"Yellowwood Park. Why are you hiding away here all alone?" She took off her watch, dipped her fingers into the sugar container and sprayed the spices over steaks stacked on a tray by the sink. The curves of her hips were wide in front of me.

"Are you shy? Scared of girls?"

"Not really. I will vibe with you, but first you must eat; after that we will chill."

"Why the naughty smile, then?"

"Nothing."

"You are a crook; all shy men are crooks. I have brothers, you know. I grew up with boys."

Zandile turned her head and caught my shameless stare—intense and undisturbed—at the rounded mounds of her ass and hips. My eyes locked with hers. The corners of her lips began to stretch into a smile. She turned away, back to the spices and meat.

"Bring the meat when you are done. I'll be in the back making the fire. Here is a chair if you'd like to sit."

"Thanks," Zandile said, without a glance at me.

I picked up a bag of charcoal from the cupboard under the sink, next to the case of whiskey. I slowly exited through the kitchen door, reluctant to lose sight of the view. Zandile ignored the chair. Generous with spices, she had coated the fillet steaks to a coarse light brown, as if they were sprinkled with sand. She leaned over the sink and washed her hands. Bottom heavy, her hips and ass stood out. I headed for the backyard and imagined the crazy things my hands and tongue could do to Zandile's curves if given the chance.

The charcoal was the quick-lighting type; I did not even open the bag, but just tossed it on the braai stand and lit the corner with a match. The flames ate up the flimsy cover and the bricks of charcoal caught fire instantly. I felt the chill in the air, then remembered the case of whiskey in the kitchen.

Zandile was not there. I placed my set—glass, whiskey bottle, still mineral water, apple juice and ice cubes—on the kitchen chair. The sound of the bass from the music system was laced with chatter from the lounge. In the backyard, I poured a drink and sat down next to the smoky braai stand. I took a sip and stood up to check the charcoal. Zandile approached with a large pot.

"Be fast, but by that I do not mean we want the meat raw."

She placed the pot next to the chair. Our eyes locked again in a steady stare. She smiled and turned away. Zandile was heavy-set, but her walk to the kitchen was light-footed, effortless. At the door she turned and caught my gaze. She smiled.

"After I eat, will you pour me a shot of your whiskey? I just want one shot to chase the cold out."

"Whisky!"

"Yes, whiskey. Are you surprised that I drink whiskey?"

"No, it is just that there are so many other ways to warm the body. Coffee, a heater, a blanket and..."

"And what?"

"You know the last one is the best of all."

"Which is...?"

She stood at the kitchen door—one leg inside, the rest of her in a pose under the outside light, illuminated for my viewing pleasure.

"You know the one, where two bodies warm each other."

Zandile burst into a laugh, her eyes on mine. "See, I told you quiet men are crooks."

She disappeared into the kitchen, her surprised giggle still in the air. I drank whiskey while the meat sizzled.

When all the meat was done, I took the pot to the kitchen. Zandile and two of her friends had chopped, sliced and diced lettuce, onions, green pepper and carrots into two large bowls. Their eyes were heavy on my back when I followed the bass into the lounge.

The sofas in the lounge were spread out, the coffee table lost to the balcony. The Tongaat crew had turned the space in the center into a dance floor. Muted music videos played on the television.

Musa and a crew of three guys huddled on the balcony, whiskey and glasses atop the displaced coffee table. I joined them but thought myself too drunk; they were talking in whispers under the bass line but apparently understood each other, for they nodded, laughed, took fives. Musa did not bother with introductions. To my whiskied eyes, it looked like business. A sip from my glass delivered only ice cubes. My set was by the braai stand. I peeled away to base but found it chilly, the heat of the fire gone, cremation of the charcoal complete. The heavy load of fatigue on my shoulders had returned. I picked up the set, ghosted past the lounge and released a torrent into the toilet. I went into the bedroom. Sprawled on the bed, I called Nana.

"Hey, baby. How are you?"

"Sleepy. How did it go at the funeral?"

"All right. When can I see you?"

"Why? Do you miss me?"

"You know I do," I said.

"Tomorrow is out 'cause I will be in church. You know how strict Ma is about church and the Sunday lunch afterwards."

"Monday, then. I will take you to school."

"Be early, baby, because I am writing a test during the second period. I have to be in class by nine at least."

"What time should I pick you up?"

"With the extra traffic of Monday, make it seven o'clock. I will wait for you at the bus stop."

"All right, baby, I was just checking on you. Goodnight."

"Goodnight. Text me something nice."

"You said you were sleeping; you will be dreaming by the time I send it. You know I am not good with messages."

"You are starting it again. Baby, I sleep on the same pillow with my phone. I will hear the message tone and read it. I would not ask for your texts if I did not like them."

"All right, I will send, but don't expect a poem."

"I'll be waiting, won't sleep till I get it. Love you, goodnight."

I poured whiskey and struggled with the buttons on my phone. My mind went blank, then drifted off on a tangent. I thought of the show we had pulled at Vusi's funeral. Stunt driving, orange flames, burning tires, the works. Strangely enough, there were no blue skies or distant horizons to gaze at in my recollection of the funeral of a natural. White smoke from the spinning tires of the VR6 and the spectacular balls of fire were suspended in a light red dust cloud. It was the same red as the earth we had piled over Vusi's casket. I snapped out of it and took a sip from my sweaty glass. I settled on something basic, wrote "I love you" and sent the message to Nana.

I lay on my back on the bed, eyes closed. After years of practice, I could locate the load of fatigue above my shoulder blades. The lump was pronounced over my left shoulder, so I shifted the weight of my body. Like a balloon bursting in slow motion, the load deflated. With each fraction lost, bit by bit I crawled into slumber, into the blank canvas of dreamless sleep.

❖

I heard a distant, hollow whistle. It was like a switch that set images in motion on the blank canvas. The fatigue was back, but was now a fluid mass inside my chest. On the canvas appeared a cross section of my ribcage. The contents of my chest looked like wet, unfloated concrete. At a distant whistle, the cartilage of my sternum cracked. I stood up and the concrete load gushed down to my pelvic and leg bones.

Swallowed into the canvas, I grimaced as concrete took over my leg bones and dried instantly. Out of thin air, a full-length mirror flashed for an instant. In the reflection, my legs and thighs became swollen from within, the muscles and veins defined, my abdomen unchanged, the bottom half a mass of muscle—like a brown-skinned Incredible Hulk. At the sound of the whistle close by, I looked around and recognized my surroundings as Musa's lounge.

My first step on concrete bones was accompanied by a scream that hurt my already cracked sternum, but was in all honesty muted from within. Only the whistle was amplified in the weird hush. Wet tar rained from the ceiling. By the fourth step, I was ankle deep in a greasy black mass. My concrete bones were heavy, but my bulky legs made light work of it all. Through the glass of the sliding door, I saw droplets of black rain—a lighter version of the sticky mass on the floor.

I managed to trace the origins of the whistle to the backyard. Glossy tar trickled out of the walls of the passageway and doorless kitchen.

The backyard was knee deep in a river of tar. From the heavens fell droplets of black drizzle. The whistle fell silent. On the spot where I had sat next to the braai stand, a figure sat in a chair with his back to me. I wiped the tar from my eyelashes. A bald scalp and arms on armrests were the only parts visible over the high back of the chair. I removed more tar from my eyelashes and nostrils.

With only two steps to touch, my step faltered. My concrete bones grew heavier, my bulky muscles tired. I looked down to find the river of tar waist high. I summoned all the power in me. It was then that I was blinded by the glow of white sunshine. A radiant ball of white pierced through the tar rain and instantly dried the river of tar. I was buried from the waist down. The chair shifted.

It was Vusi, untouched by the tar rain. He was in the clothes we had buried him in. His smile flashed without any gold. The two knives buried with him were clutched in his hands. His smile turned to disgust.

"Sipho!" he shouted.

Vusi had somehow grown taller. I looked up at him. "Catch!" he said.

It was yellow spit, a substance that, bar the color, had all the moves of quicksilver. It fell in front of me, splintered, then gelled. The gob sped around me in two rapid circles to rest as an arrow that pointed to the side. It slowed to the point of the arrow and settled first yellow, then clear. It turned into a picture.

A projected and magnified photo formed the new

canvas. I was swallowed by it too, sucked out of dry tar to stand at the base of a canvas as wide as the sky. It was clear and bright. Shacks on a slope formed the top half of the canvas. At the bottom left corner sat the rusted chassis of a car. The ear of a green enamel cup on top of a block was at the bottom right corner. More blocks in the space between. Over them, a cigarette was snug between the fingers of what was definitely my grease-covered hand. It was the picture of the backyard at home. I looked back, but Vusi was gone.

i HEARD THE TRUTH iN PiETERMARiTZBURG

My eyes opened to the ceiling in the bedroom. It was spotless and solid white. I scanned every inch of it, but there were no traces of tar. I ran my fingers down my chest and touched where—in the dream—my sternum had cracked. I found my ribcage and its contents intact, but coughed just to make sure. Air from deep in my lungs rushed out in free flow.

There was a peculiar lightness to my body. The load was gone, shed somewhere in dreamland. I had fallen asleep fully dressed. I sat up with ease and rolled up my pants to the knees; a fleeting glance revealed limbs shrunk, undefined, normal. My set was on the stand next to the bed.

Though light of body and perfect of breath, there was a persistent dryness in my throat. What I needed was cold water. I took a sip from the bowl of melted ice cubes. The water was at room temperature—warm on the tongue—and seemed to evade all the dry spots as it went down.

The freakish buoyancy of my body took some getting used to. It was at the opposite end of the scale to the struggles across the slushy tar river in my dream. I stood still for a minute, light as a feather, my eyes on the ceramic floor tiles. My first few steps were tentative, infantile and overthought.

Out of the window, the sky was dark and brooding. Not exactly tar-rain black, but close enough. Dense, gunmetal-gray clouds sat stubbornly on the horizon. At a glance, my forecast for the day was zero sunshine.

I went down the passageway, my hands against the walls for balance. With every second step, a weird feeling of weightlessness took over and I had to hold on to something. My fingers felt the walls for tar. The cream paint on the walls was velvety to the eye but smooth like plastic to touch. My fingers were clean. I opened the door to Musa's room.

Musa was already gone. The only keys on the stand next to his bed were for the 325is. A chilly wind blasted through the windows left open to clear out the scent of sex, alcohol, cigarettes and weed. The scent combo was light when I entered, almost negligible in the cold air. I closed the windows and opened Musa's wardrobe in search of something warm.

Designer jackets too expensive to share with even a blood relative made up most of the warm clothes department. I jumped over ten of the jackets to the sweaters. I skipped over a handful of the sweaters, for many still had price tags under the collars, to an old Adidas hoodie. I recalled how Musa had tried to sell me the hoodie when it was new, along with a Diesel watch; it was among the first items he ever shoplifted. I pulled the sweater off the hanger, but it slipped right through my hands to crumple over shoe boxes at the bottom of the wardrobe.

For all his casual dress sense, Musa loved his shoes with a passion. He kept them all in their original boxes. I moved the sweater to the side and counted twelve boxes. Three Hugo Boss black label, four Hugo Boss orange label, one Armani, two Versace, with Adidas and Nike making up the remaining two. From the price tags stuck to the sides of the boxes, I calculated them to be enough for a deposit on a brand-new German sedan. I went through all the shoe boxes—each still had the paper padding and pouch of salts from the store.

The shoes with the simplest of designs—Armani and Hugo Boss black label—were little worn, the soles relatively clean. The outlandish Hugo Boss orange labels and peacock patterns of Versace had slightly more mileage. The Adidas sneakers were brand-new.

Dazed in the haze of lightness, I picked up what I at first reckoned to be the heaviest pair of sneakers Nike ever made. I opened the box, peeling away the paper covering; in the center of the shoebox sat a silver Colt .45 pistol, the pouch of salts at the end of the barrel. My mind cut to the night in KwaMashu when Sibani unloaded the magazine of an identical weapon into another man's head. And the sound it made—like a thunderstorm heard full blast through top-of-the-range earphones—was just as loud even in the recollection. The desert that was my throat snapped me out of the flashback. I closed the box and picked up the Adidas hoodie. When I closed the door to Musa's room, I thought: What if a bullet ever really was only a pouch of salts?

❖

The clean-up after the party was nothing short of meticulous. A solitary empty cider bottle, missed because it was in a corner behind a sofa, was the only evidence there had been a party. The sofas were still spread out; the coffee table now stood just inside the partially open sliding door. The gap in the sliding door let in the cold whistling wind. I closed it and put on the hoodie. I watched the trees buck in the wind until the drought in my throat returned. I poured half a glass of chilled water from the fridge in the kitchen, topping it up with tap water. I peeked at the backyard through the kitchen door. Stuck in admiration of the colors—the dark gray of the sky and rich green of the grass—I drifted and thought of the fly outfit that could come out of it all if ever the colors were translated into fabric. Two black refuse bags filled with empty bottles sat on either side of the garbage bin by the door. The cold wind pricked my face. I closed the kitchen door.

The pot with the meat from the party was in the fridge. I tilted the lid and estimated that only half of the steaks had been eaten. Of the two salad bowls prepared, one was untouched. I poured another mix of chilled and tap water. In the lounge I called Musa.

"Awake at last. What happened to you?"

"I don't know. I think I was just tired. Are you off to Tongaat?"

"For sure."

I heard girls greet in the background. "The girls say 'hi,'" he shouted.

"Listen, Musa, I have to tell you about this dream I had."

"I'll call you later—cops ahead. I can't get another ticket for using a cellphone while driving. Call you later."

I sank into the sofa, remote control in hand,

skipped over all the channels and settled on music videos. Tattoos, supercars, girls with fat asses, diamond teeth, watches and chains—it was hip-hop hour. I sipped from the glass and just looked at the excess, the gleaming gloating of the have-nots when they finally have. Every frame was staged to flatter, bass lines dominant yet contained, the rest— guitars, pianos, flutes and such—sparse and faint. In my mind, it all needed something extra. A bit of strings, more keys and flutes. I wished there was more, more fire to the movement where, at the least, four instruments collided on my eardrums to tell the same tale, in different ways, simultaneously. Vocally, only two MCs genuinely flowed. The rest made words rhyme by force. I turned down the volume.

The bell of the intercom was yet another beat without atmosphere. Placed the coffee table in its rightful place and rushed to peek through the window next to the intercom. At the gate was a small white van, the back filled with spray-painting equipment. I buzzed the gate open.

Two men were in a Ford Bantam. The passenger door opened and one stepped out. He was of stocky build, but when he stood up, I saw how tall he was— mountainous, his waist in line with the roof of the van. He looked to be in his early thirties; when he stretched his arms and extended even further, I wondered how he had ever fitted into the vehicle. A full, hearty smile flashed across his face when I shook his enormous hand.

The driver did not stop to shake hands, but offloaded the equipment. He was of slighter build, maybe a decade older, and shorter.

He had glassy red eyes and an inanimate face, as if the muscles of his cheeks, forehead and jaw were carved from stone. Even when he held a lighted cigarette in his mouth, his lips remained still.

Their overalls indicated the nature of their work. Originally blue, they were splattered with layers of white, navy, maroon, silver and yellow paint. I led them to the garage.

"If we are to move freely, move this other car for us." Stoneface pointed to the 325is. I rushed to Musa's room.

On returning to the garage with the keys for the 325is, I found the painters caressing my 328i. Inch by inch, they felt over the body of the car—all signs of its original green color covered under a coat of gray primer applied a few days earlier. The painters each carried white chalk as they inspected the light gray surface. They made tiny white crosses on areas deemed too rough to touch.

I reversed the 325is out of the garage and sparked a cigarette by the gate. The clouds were a darker shade of the gray primer on my 328i. Drizzle in the distance formed a misty curtain to the horizon. Back in the garage, the inspection went on in silence. The painters' heads seemed almost glued to their hands, their ears close to the body of the car, as if listening for the rough patches. To break the silence with conversation was to disturb. I took a shower, but every time I blinked at the shower head it seemed to ooze shiny black tar. My hooded reflection in the mirror made me realize that I was low in the sportswear department. I also felt like taking a drive. The notes in my back pocket made R700 and some change.

In the garage, the giant painter was on a ladder, his head above the base of the roof trusses. He taped a sheet of protective plastic to the garage walls. Stoneface sanded away at the white crosses. The giant on the ladder turned to acknowledge my presence; his face looked well versed in social niceties. I shouted over the ferocious sanding.

"I am off to the Pavilion, do you need anything there?"

"No, we are all right."

"There is food in the fridge if you want to eat something. I'll be back in like two hours."

"We have food; the only thing you can show us is the toilet and a place where we can smoke."

"Down the corridor, third door on your left, that's the toilet. Cigarettes you can bust on the balcony."

"All right."

"I'll be back now-now," I said.

Out of the gate, I looked at the approaching rain and reaffirmed that the sun was definitely not coming out. I was easy on the 325is, mellow like the Sunday morning songs on the radio. By the time I got to fifth gear, I was tired of the DJs' talk, and then three stations seemed to play the same song simultaneously. The only CD in the car was of house music. I played one track, but music of the night did not feel right on a Sunday morning. I switched off the stereo.

In the quiet, I realized for the first time that the Vusi in my dream was clean, yet the Vusi in my head was the bandaged boy on a metal tray in a drawer at the mortuary. Pictures of the two Vusis lingered for a few minutes, but I lit a cigarette and erased them. In the parking lot, I rushed a few puffs in the chilly breeze and disappeared into the lights of the Pavilion shopping mall.

I got there with the staff. Girls with faces recently put together. All the people who passed me were in uniform, the smell of perfume still fresh for each encounter. My hand paged through the notes in my back pocket as I window-shopped. I bought a T-shirt and track pants on sale at Sportscene, and left when couples and families began to flood into the mall.

At Musa's, the painters were on a smoke break on the balcony. I tried on the new clothes and decided to wear the T-shirt. I cleaned up the set on the braai stand. With the whiskey bottle and dash in hand, I stepped into the lounge with hopes of some chatter, but the smoke break was over. The balcony was empty. The sound of sandpaper on metal came from the garage. I warmed two steaks and munched down in the lounge while watching an action movie. My belly full, I dozed off in the middle of the many explosions on screen.

A giant red hand shook me awake.

"We have finished. Tomorrow around midday we'll come back to polish the car, but that will only take two hours. Till then do not open the garage at all," said the colossal painter.

I buzzed them out and stood in the cold, sheltered under the veranda, gazing at the raindrops on the 325is.

Alone, I watched a soccer match played on the greenest pitch in a stadium in England where crowds sang from beginning to end. I wished I were the one who passed and dribbled in faraway grassed operas, showing the world the skills I had learned on the dusty pitch in M Section. The post-match analysis was a bore. I called Musa.

"Howzit?" Musa shouted to drown out the background noise. "I don't know when I'll be back, but I've got another key for the gate and the house. So if you want to move around, don't worry. What are you doing over there, anyway?"

"Nothing. The painters already left. Where is your weed?"

"In the drawer of the TV stand. You can come here if you want; I'll give you directions. It is a wild party over here. Zandile was asking about you."

"I'll call you if I am coming."

"You won't regret it. Come up here, clear your head, socialize and forget about dreams."

"I'll call if I am coming. Tell Zandile I said 'hi.'"

"If you come here you can tell her yourself."

I set the alarm on my phone for six in the morning, smoked a blunt and slept on the sofa.

❖

"Hey, baby, how far are you?"

It was Nana, and it was six-thirty. The alarm had woken me at six, but I had switched it off and gone back to sleep.

"I am about to enter the township." I stretched on the sofa, trying to sound as awake as possible.

"In five minutes, I am leaving for the bus stop."

"I'll see you just now. The traffic is heavy here at V Section," I lied. "You know how Mondays get. Too much traffic."

"I have now stood still; there may be an accident ahead. Baby, leave for the bus stop in fifteen minutes."

"Okay, I will see you just now."

I blitzed through the shower and bombed down to the township.

At V Section, the exit lane was an ocean of stagnant traffic. On my side there was ample space to knit around the slower cars. In the entrance lane there were only a few private cars, the odd bus and a handful of taxis with music systems so powerful that when I overtook them the bass hit the center of my chest and meshed the beat of my heart with another internal organ. It was morning, but house was the music of choice. Odes to the midnight moon blasted at the sunrise. I did not envy the passengers. Schoolchildren on the pavements danced to the bass. All this told me I was home, a world away from the quiet streets of Westville.

Nana was at the bus stop with two schoolmates. She opened the door, got into the car and fixed her gaze out the passenger window.

"Don't you want to give your friends a lift?" I said.

"Why are you so concerned?"

I dismissed it as Monday blues and drove off. Her school bag was on her lap.

"You can put your bag in the back seat."

I searched for her eyes. They were somewhere out the passenger window. We hit traffic on the freeway. I moved from lane to lane in search of flow.

"It's no use overtaking—we are in traffic. You can change lanes but they all stall in the end. You will cause an accident instead," Nana said.

"Are you angry at me or something?"

"No."

On the radio, the morning shows were all in talk,

talk, talk mode. Nana shook her head when I lit a cigarette.

For the first time that morning I saw that her eyes and face were drenched in distress. Without me uttering a word, she said, "How dare you?"

"Baby, what is wrong?"

I dragged one more pull and tossed the cigarette out the window. "Nothing," she said and looked away.

"Then why the attitude? It is not like you will be late for your test."

We exited the freeway.

"That has nothing to do with it."

"What, then?"

Her stare was straight ahead.

"People talk, you know. Everything you do gets back to me. If you do things, I will know."

"What are you talking about?"

"Saturday, you spun and burned a car at the funeral. My friends saw you there. I wonder what is going on with you, Sipho."

"So? I was saying goodbye to a friend. What is wrong with that?"

"You think I don't know, baby. Car thieves spin cars at funerals for car thieves."

At the robots, I glanced out the window. From the corner of my eye I saw how she looked at me. The lights did not turn green fast enough. I looked straight ahead, at first avoiding eye contact, then irked by how softly I conceded and gave her my eyes.

"Do you steal cars now?"

Her face was the picture of genuine anger, but her eyes begged me to say no. The green light bailed me out.

"Like I said, baby, I was saying goodbye to a friend. I don't steal cars, I just know how to spin, that's all."

"I don't like this new friend of yours. This Musa is changing you."

"I don't like your friends either. They are putting ideas into your head, and you believe them. How can I steal? Who will kiss you when I am in jail?"

"Of all the things you can do, stealing is the most stupid. Thieves always get caught. If you are, that will be the end of us."

Nana's unconvincing threat bounced off me. We parked in a bay by the gate at her school.

"I'll pick you up after school."

"Don't bother. My mother is fetching me."

"What is wrong?"

"Nothing is wrong. Where are you going now?"

"Home. I have a lot of cars to fix."

"Call me at break time."

"What time is your break time?"

"Ten-thirty."

"For sure. Write well."

"Thanks."

She stepped out of the car.

I watched her until she disappeared in a sea of similar uniforms. On the freeway, I plastered the 325is to the tarmac and followed the information boards to Pietermaritzburg.

The clouds pulled a disappearing act just before I reached the Marianhill tollgate. The sun came out and shimmered in all its glorious splendor. I opened the sunroof and embraced the morning rays. My foot was timid on the accelerator pedal, and I let the 325is rumble effortlessly at the speed limit.

I filled the tank at a garage in Camperdown and ordered takeaway—a cheap burger, chips and cold drink combo. I smoked a pencil blunt behind the garage, then picked up the food order and chilled in the car. I washed down the blunt with half the cold drink and called Uncle Stan.

"Hey, nephew, is everything all right? It is not every day that I hear from you."

"Everything is okay, Uncle Stan. I am calling about that thing we talked about where I was to get some know-how from you."

"Oh! That thing. Where are you?"

"Camperdown."

"My day is really hectic. I am leaving for a meeting in the city, but in two hours I will be finished. I'll call you then."

I ate the meal and washed it down with the remainder of the cold drink. Outside the garage, I smoked the mandatory after-meal cigarette and eased on to Pietermaritzburg. When I got there, I parked at the first garage. The 325is was next in line at the car wash at the back. Opposite the garage was a one-floor shopping mall; I killed time with magazines in a CNA.

"Where are you now?"

"At the first mall when you enter the city, Uncle Stan."

"Wait for me at the Spur across from that mall. I'll be there in ten minutes."

I sat at a table with a view of the Spur parking lot. I flipped through the morning paper I picked up on entering and located the sports section. It was close to midday and the sun was hot. A plump, light-skinned waitress approached with the menu.

"Here is the menu. Would you like something to drink while you decide?"

"Give me a Coke."

"Regular or mega?"

"Regular."

"Coming right up," she said.

I did not even pretend to read the menu. I read the sports section, occasionally looking up at the end of a paragraph. The Coke arrived.

"Have you decided what to eat?"

"Not yet. Give me a minute."

The waitress shifted to another table—an old white couple who were in the middle of a massive brunch. I sipped Coke into my already full stomach. I looked up and saw a navy S500 Mercedes-Benz ease into the parking lot. Uncle Stan got out of the driver's side. He was in elegant casual: white linen shirt, beige linen pants and brown suede loafers. He greeted the waitresses with familiarity.

"Hey, nephew, how are you? Every time I see you, you are taller."

"I am okay, Uncle Stan. How are they at home?"

"They are okay. Have you ordered?"

"I am not hungry. When I called you, I was eating."

"I am famished. There was no time for breakfast when I left home in the morning."

He called the waitress and ordered a breakfast combo, complete with mega orange juice. Our meeting started off with general chatter. He did not see a bright future for the national soccer team. Grassroots player development and general lack of ambition was the problem. The heat I was complaining about was nothing compared to what they had the previous day.

"So, nephew, tell me about this thing that has brought you to Pietermaritzburg, after...how long has it been? Five years since you were last here."

"I have this friend, Uncle Stan, who gets Mandrax pills at a good price. He has put me on, but I have never moved pills before. What I need from you is some know-how."

"Is it a good pill, though?"

"The thick white boss."

"That is a good pill. First rule is that your product must be quality. Druggies won't buy it if it is shit. Remember you sell to people whose lives revolve around getting high. They may look like shit, but they won't buy your pills if they are shit. But before we even get to that, first things first. Who is this friend of yours?"

His food arrived. Uncle Stan thanked the waitress. His nose, lips and the faint creases at the corners of his eyes were exactly like my mother's.

"The reason I ask, nephew, is that in this game, police informants are planted everywhere."

"Mdala is my connect."

"Mdala from J Section? The one with the taxis?"

"Yes."

"I know him. I did a lot of good business with him back in the day."

Uncle Stan munched down. I forced sips of Coke down my throat.

"The money part I will not tell you about because I am sure you understand it, otherwise you would not be sitting here with me, talking business."

"There is mad money in this thing, Uncle Stan, and

I want in."

"True, there is mad money in this, but mad men as well. People who will smile in your face but plot your downfall behind your back. Bad men who will force you to prove how serious you are about this money. Men who will not pay you your money. Are you ready to prove that you want this money? That is the question you must ask yourself before you even start. Otherwise it will all be in vain."

"I have people, Uncle Stan; no one will hustle me. Of that I am sure."

"But they will try."

Just like Ma and Nu, Uncle Stan was a steady eater. For each mouthful, his fork impaled tiny pieces of each item on the plate.

"This thing is tricky, nephew. The game is tricky— I won't lie to you. For one thing, I cannot give you pointers because you will be moving it in Durban and I no longer have connections in the game down there. And in this thing, you must make decisions on your own. It is a brutal game; I wonder why you are choosing it. I have seen many people fizzle out in this game. Some were unlucky, others were simply not cut out for this. Some, like me, make it.

"Here lies the gist of this thing, nephew. The only way to find out if drug dealing is your thing is to do it. If it suits you, cash will fall like raindrops. But otherwise jail or death are the soldiers of the end game. I know scores of dealers dying in jail. Though drug dealing was not for them, dying in jail is a sad way of finding that out."

He washed down the meal with orange juice and set his plate and glass aside.

"What about school? Did you ever go back?"

"I did not learn anything there, Uncle Stan."

"And cars?"

"I still fix cars from home, but it is slow."

"I want you to digest what I told you about the game for a few days and call me on Friday. I will give you pointers then but it will be general things—what to look out for and what not to do."

"Thanks, Uncle Stan."

"I am off to another meeting."

"You are busy, Uncle Stan."

"In this life, you have to be. If all goes well in this meeting, I will be through with drugs. I want to open a tire fitment center here in the city. I just recently realized that there is more money in rubber than in pills. I'll hear from you on Friday; if not, I will organize some work for you if my deal pans out. It won't be crazy drug money, but you will live."

I watched my mother's brother as he left—cellphone to his ear as he opened the Benz's door, reversed and disappeared. I finished the Coke, paid for his meal, slid into the 325is and followed the information boards back to Durban.

I stopped at a garage near Hammarsdale. All the cold drinks played havoc with my bladder. My hands were under the hand drier in the toilet when Musa called.

"Howzit?"

"Sharp. Where are you?"

"Near Hammarsdale."

"What are you doing there?"

"I had to see my Uncle Stan up in Pietermaritzburg."

"Did he have good news?"

"Yes, but also a bit of bad news. He preached a lot."

"The painters finished polishing your car."

"How did it come out?"

"Shiny red. It is beautiful. You can sell it today if you want; it is irresistible."

"I'll be there in an hour."

"Hurry down here; the ecstasy package has also arrived."

My reflection in the mirror of the garage toilets stared back at me. I took a few steps for a closer look. From ear to ear, a dry, joyless grin was on my face.

PiLLARS OF SAND

I plastered the 325is onto the fast lane from the moment I left the garage. Musa's call injected urgency after Uncle Stan's lecture. Traffic on the freeway was sparse; there were stretches where the rear-view mirror showed three vacant lanes. The image was out of focus at the base of the reflection—distorted by thin vapor steaming off the tarmac.

At the bends near Hammarsdale, I crept behind a yellow dolphin-shaped M3 but lost ground when I upscaled the curves. My foot pressed the accelerator pedal to the floor. The 325is screamed out at maximum revs, yet the yellow M3 just climbed and climbed. In seconds, the gap between us widened substantially.

On the downward side, the yellow dolphin eased down. From a distance, it looked like a yellow arrow that grew as I slithered behind it. It set the pace for the remainder of the journey, and I stayed in its slipstream until the Westville off-ramp.

Musa was on the balcony, bare-chested. It was not as hot as in Pietermaritzburg, but he wore only cargo pants. A cigarette sat tilted on his lips. I approached the balcony to greet him and bum a cigarette. He pointed to the garage.

"I know you can't wait—go on," he said. I ran to

the garage and opened the door.

Glossy cherry red was the new color of my once-green BMW 328i. It was good enough to drive—the engine number, tags and ignition changed. I ran my hand over the front fender like a seasoned paint inspector: smooth, no air bubbles. The light in the garage came on. My reflection off the red body and side windows was clear, with crispy sharpness to the edges. Musa stood next to me.

"They did a good job. What did I tell you about this money?"

"You said it, Musa. If we want it bad enough, we will get it."

Musa put his hand out. Over the handshake, our eyes met in the reflection.

"Thanks, Musa. Without you, all this would not have been possible."

"No problem, my friend. We will make more money; you haven't seen anything yet."

I moved around the car and continued to examine the paint job. "It has low mileage; you can sell it by the end of the week if you want to."

Musa switched off the lights and left the garage. I followed him out the garage door and into the lounge.

A brown parcel was on the coffee table. Musa sat down on the sofa and ripped it open. He peeled back the brown paper to reveal a white, foam-filled layer. The foam layer protected the ecstasy—tiny blue pills tightly packed in transparent plastic. He opened the plastic and freed the pills onto the table.

"How did it go in Pietermaritzburg?"

"Uncle Stan laid out the Mandrax game like it should be laid out."

"What did he tell you?"

"He told me about backstabbing and double-crossing and jail and death."

"But those are the givens in this life we have chosen."

"I think he was trying to be an uncle, that's all."

"This pack should have one thousand pills. We have half each, so start counting your share," Musa said.

We counted in silence. I counted mine in tens and grouped the pills in piles of hundreds. On pill number 260, a text message alert tone shook the phone in the pocket of my track pants. The message was from Nana: "Thanx 4 callin 8 breaktym." Before I could press the green button to call her, my phone rang. I did not recognize the number.

"Young blood."

"Long time, Mdala. How are you?"

"Forget about how I am. The package has arrived. Meet me in the city around eight. Call this number when you get to Point Road."

"Sure, Mdala. That is good news." He hung up.

"It is all good news for you today. Look at you beaming; you can't even hide your joy."

"Mdala said the Mandrax game is on."

"You are in serious money now, Sipho."

We counted five hundred pills each. Five hundred tiny azure tablets with a defined diamond stamped on one side. The pills lay on the coffee table in two tiny heaps of blue. Fifteen extra pills and a few broken pieces were surplus to the pack. Musa shifted the broken pieces to my share and put the extras into a plastic coin bag. He tossed the bag from hand to hand and juggled it in the air. The bag came to rest on one hand. Musa dangled it, moving his hand back and forth; my eyes were hypnotized by a pendulum of blue pills.

"Fifteen extra pills. Did I tell you about the party in Umhlanga?" Musa said.

"No, you didn't."

"There is a party there today. A perfect place for us to introduce these blue diamonds."

"When is it going down?"

"After nine or something like that."

"I'll meet you there. I need to go home; I haven't seen them in a while."

I shifted my share to the edge of the coffee table and let the pills fall into a transparent Ziploc bag. I put the broken pieces in the back pocket of my track pants. In the garage, I deflated the spare tire of my red Beemer and placed my share of the ecstasy inside it.

We shared a blunt on the balcony. The late nights, rather than the potency of the weed, rushed Musa off to slumberland. I shook him awake when he started to snore. He did not say a word, but rose, half asleep, and trudged to his bedroom.

I watched a movie to its happy ending and instantly forgot it. It was dark outside by the time the credits rolled. I did what I had been itching to do from the moment I arrived from Pietermaritzburg. I grabbed the keys for the 328i from the TV stand.

"I am off," I shouted by the closed door of Musa's room.

"Call when you get to the Gateway shopping mall. I will come and meet you."

The smell of leather filled my nostrils. I sank into the bucket seat and moved it all the way back. I turned the key and set the headlight switch to dim. The dashboard came to life. The odometer read 32 654 kilometers. The fuel gauge was just below full. My middle finger popped the gear lever to neutral and I started the car. A deep rumble bounced off the garage walls. I pressed the gear knob down to reverse and set all the mirrors.

When I reversed, the cabin fell silent. It was as if I had left the rumble in the garage. I pressed hard as I meandered out of Westville. Still there was no rumble.

On the freeway it was even more bizarre; the speedometer needle was on 160 km/h, and I kept passing cars, but the cabin seemed soundproof. I opened the window and pressed harder. The speedometer and rev counter needles went haywire. The rumble I so wanted came in the form of a kick dead center at the back of my waist.

I shoved my red glider with disregard for bends. Miserly on the brake pedal, I followed the white lines, my foot down on the accelerator—particularly on curves. I made the decision that the following day I would fill the tank, thrash it down to Port Shepstone, buy a packet of cigarettes and come back.

I hit the evening township traffic just as the car started to warm.

It was my first time in a car that new. My honest opinion was that the previous owner had been too easy on it. Constrained breathing out the exhaust pipes drowned out the rumble. It was nothing that the morning dash to Port Shepstone wouldn't fix. My plan was to clock it at least four times for aural augmentation. I inched home in traffic and parked behind two other cars at Mama Mkhize's Tavern. The few patrons at Mama Mkhize's were inside the house. When I killed the engine, I could hear jazz playing at low volume, laced with barely discernible chatter. I finished the rest of my journey home on foot and disappeared into the smothering darkness of 2524 Close, my road of eternally dark streetlights.

From a distance, the night veiled the blue wall in black. Then the bright lights of a matchbox BMW 320i flashed across and made it blue. It was the boyfriend of our neighbor's daughter. He made a U-turn at the ring. I rushed to the gap in the blue wall. The white BMW parked at the neighbor's gate and the driver made a call. His girlfriend was not home, for he shook his head and sped off. The strays disguised as pets were not at the gap in the blue wall.

My father was on a bench below the outside light by the kitchen door. He was washing his hands in a bucket. The contents were a mixture of dishwasher soap, water, a dash of paint thinner, powdered soap and a pinch of back-yard sand. It was thanks to this concoction that I never had mechanic's hands.

Maybe it was the shadows made by the outside light on my father's face. He was as meticulous as ever while he washed his hands, but that night I saw a frailty to his outline, a slowness to the whole process.

"How are you, Dad?"

"How are you, Sipho?"

"All right and busy. If we had a workshop, we'd make a killing; the customers Musa brings have no stories. They pay what you charge."

"Musa?"

"He knows people with cars, Dad."

By the concrete sink next to the bench, my father rinsed his hands. Shoulders slumped, he was the picture of exhaustion. The stiffness against which he moved seemed to emanate from within, as if it was actually the bones in him that were weary. I followed him into the house.

"Your mother so wanted to see you."

"What about?"

"She said she missed you."

"It is not like I have been away for months, Dad. It was just a few days."

"You know your mother; when you were a kid, she missed you even if you were playing in the backyard."

Dad picked up his supper and a newspaper from the kitchen table.

Nu was in front of the TV in the lounge. Thumb in mouth, she nodded in and out of sleep.

"I have been telling her for an hour to go to bed." Dad sat down on the sofa with his supper.

I shook Nu. She opened her bloodshot eyes, smiled from the depths of a dream and went back to sleep.

"Nu!" Dad shouted.

She rose, thumb in mouth, eyes closed, and disappeared into the bedroom. Nu also slept in our parents' room, just as I had until she was born.

Dad ate his supper, looking bored by a dance show in the slot before the news. He flipped through the newspaper. I washed his plate and withdrew R500 from my bank under the mattress in my room. Dad was asleep when the news started, his head slumped behind the newspaper. The editorial page had sent him to sleep. Creases of age ran wild over his tranquil face. Children grow, parents age. Mdala called.

"Where are you now?" he barked over the phone.
"I am leaving the township," I said.

"How can you drag your feet for cash? Are you still interested?"

"For sure, Mdala."

"Around eight means five minutes before and five minutes after."

"It is twenty minutes to eight now."

"I won't wait for you if you are later than five past."

"Don't worry, Mdala, I will be there at five to."

I sent my father to bed and lit a cigarette in the backyard, my gaze resting on the dimly lit shacks of Power.

My eyes wandered. I scanned my neighborhood. In the darkest corner of the yard, at the home of my friend Sticks, there was a silhouette of two people kissing: Sticks and the neighbor's daughter. I slid into my shiny cherry-red glider.

I was in cruise mode but still made it to the city on time. I reserved my speeding for the following morning. In thirteen minutes, I was rolling down the empty streets of Durban at night, when all the visitors were gone, and the real residents of the city roamed. A few streets before Point Road, I called Mdala's number.

"Young blood."

"Sure, Mdala, where are you?"

"Let's meet up at Battery Beach in five minutes."

I rolled down my window when I hit Point Road, easy on my red glider. Tertiary students who lived in the numerous flats of Point Road loitered on the pavements. Drunk men laughed at prostitutes, and others negotiated deals at the doors of neon-lit escort agencies. Tuck shops, bars, a queue at a shop with public phones—Point Road had a township feel. There was even the scent of weed in the air. Bar the smell of the ocean, the whorehouses and the high-rises, Monday night on Point Road was exactly like my township on a Saturday night.

I parked at Battery Beach and waited for Mdala. In the quest for the rumble of my red glider, I had not had time to get acquainted with the factory-fitted stereo. The glow of a half-moon shimmered off the ocean. I closed the window and pumped up the volume until the bass was unbearable on my eardrums.

The stereo needed nothing extra. I was satisfied with the bass. I switched it off, rolled down the window and lit a cigarette. My eyes drifted to the shiny black body of water lit by the moon. Far ahead in the deep, the ocean moved with the viscosity of oil. There was a tap on the passenger window. A full grin was on Mdala's face. I unlocked the door.

"Good to see you moving up, young blood."

"I am trying, Mdala."

"This is a beautiful car."

"Yes, the painters did a good job."

"Fresh too. Don't burn the leather with cigarettes."

"I want to sell it within the week, Mdala. If you know a buyer, I'll pay you a commission."

"I'll ask around."

The Mandrax was inside his jacket.

"Here it is. This is a pack, one thousand pills. You take your share off the top and return to me what is due."

"Seven grand," I said.

"That is right."

I placed the Mandrax pack under my seat.

"Where is Musa? I called him but I only get his voicemail," said Mdala.

The grin on his face had evaporated.

"He is at a party in Umhlanga; maybe his battery is out or something."

"Tell him to call me. When you see him, tell him it is urgent. Tell him that the Cold Hearts are back in town."

Mdala got out and disappeared into the night.

I rolled down the streets of Durban extra slow. A youngish couple crossed the street hand in hand at a red light. I called Nana.

Her voice sounded broken, like she had been crying for a long time.

"What is wrong?" I asked.

"Nothing."

"Where are you?"

"Can't talk to you now, Sipho. I'll call you tomorrow."

She hung up. Her voicemail answered the numerous calls I made after that, but I did not leave a message.

Musa's call shifted my mood from the gloom produced by Nana's broken voice—I gave up on her for the night. Musa was shouting over high-tempo house music and the chants that girls add to house tracks. Girls in Durban remix house songs with chants.

"Where are you?" he shouted.

"Leaving the city. I'll be at the Gateway in ten minutes. Where should I wait for you?"

"Park at the garage with Steers. I'll meet you there."

Charmed by the cruising abilities of my 328i, I took the longest route to the Gateway mall. I rolled along at the speed limit. The red glider was so quiet that at times I had to check the rev counter; from the sound-proof cabin I could not tell if it was even idling.

My big toe just rested on the accelerator pedal. Power was there and on cue, but I was easy on it and let it roll on in effortless glide. There were no CDs in the car, so I cruised to the sounds of night radio. I heard a rock song with the most liberated of beats on 5fm. My toe pressed a tad harder on the pedal.

I knew Musa would be late for our meeting at the Gateway garage, so I stopped at a garage off the freeway. My bladder was about to burst. The aroma of fried chips ambushed me on my way to the toilet. Maybe it was the weed we had smoked at Musa's, but I instantly felt hunger pangs. I ordered a large portion of chips and a can of Coke.

"Are you there?"

"No. Five minutes. I'll be there," I said.

"I'm leaving for the Gateway garage too now. The girls here are pretty, and they love the blue diamonds. You'll see how they dance, my friend."

I collected my order and sat in the garage parking lot, flavoring the chips and setting them out so they would be easy to eat while I drove.

I was in high spirits on the last stretch to the Gateway. In my head I compiled a movie trailer for the night I was about to play. About a kilometer from the mall, a flashing blue light filled my rear-view mirror.

A police car was behind me, right on my bumper. My heart skipped beats from my stomach, and my intestines coiled into knots. In my head there was a picture of me explaining about the ecstasy package in the spare tire I had not re-inflated, plus the one thousand Mandrax pills under my seat.

I tried to stay calm. I did not lose my pose—no sudden movements. I relaxed and drove on at a constant speed. I thought that acting calm and collected would shake them off, but it only brought on their siren. A glance in the rear-view mirror revealed two beefy white cops filling the cabin of a white unmarked Chevy SS Lumina. Another blue light flashed next to my door. An Indian cop had his hand out the passenger window of a black anaconda BMW 330i. He searched for my eyes. When he located them, his hand casually waved me to the yellow lane.

I thought of making a run for it. The beat of my heart was nomadic and out of rhythm. First in the pit of my stomach, it jumped to the right side of my chest, then to the left. My big toe twitched lightly on the brake pedal and I pulled over.

Their attack formation was executed with lightning speed. Reflected in the side-view mirrors, the two white cops approached, their guns out. In front of the bonnet, the Indian cop crouched with a rifle pointed at me. A burly forearm bristling with blond hair was gigantic in one mirror. By the passenger window another hefty frame stood ready to shoot.

"Switch off the engine and come out with both hands up," shouted the blond cop on my side.

I switched off the engine. His words amplified through the glass of my closed window. In that split second I heard his barked instructions loud and clear like my ears were close to a loudspeaker. The cabin was not so soundproof after all. Two pistols and a rifle were locked onto me. My heart churned beats from all over my abdomen. The hooves of a thousand horses stomped from within. I opened my door.

"Do you have a weapon on you?"

"No, sir," I said.

"Hands up! I said, 'Hands up!'"

I extended my already stretched hands further and stepped out of the car. Subjected to a frantic but thorough search, my legs spread, I leaned face first on the side of my glider. The blond cop missed the broken pieces of ecstasy in my back pocket. My hands were flat on the roof, like I was hugging the car, then my arms were contorted back and handcuffed. With ease, he pushed me to the tarmac in front of the car.

Only the sound of passing cars and the crackling of police radios pierced the air. The weight of the blond cop resting on my back transferred through his heavy knee between my shoulder blades. The handcuffs were way too tight, especially on my right wrist— the steel cut through the skin to grind against bone.

I tried to adapt to breathing with the blond giant on my back. I closed my eyes and tumbled into a pit of longing and loss. My heart was back in place on the left side of my chest, but there was hardly a beat. A chilly breeze swept through me, the same freezing gust that had swept through me the day I found out I was a killer.

The tarmac was rough against my chest; the knee on my back was so heavy I could feel the road surface embossed on my skin.

"Whose car is this?" said the blond cop. "Mine, sir. It is a rebuild."

"We'll see."

He stepped off me. My right ear was flat on the tarmac. As cars rolled by, I took long breaths to the dreadful sound of tires on tarmac.

The boots of the cop who had secured the passenger side slowly moved around the car and skipped over me. By the driver's door he disappeared into the cabin. The blond and the Indian sat on the guardrail behind clouds of cigarette smoke. Behind them the half-moon was bright in the cloudless sky.

The boots emerged from the cabin. They belonged to an older, broad-shouldered cop. His light brown, thinning mop shaded to gray above the ears. Cool detachment filled his plump, droopy face.

"You say the car is a rebuild?" he said.

"Yes, sir, it is a rebuild."

"And where did you get money for a rebuild?"

"I am a mechanic, sir. I saved money, sir."

"We'll see, mechanic."

He opened the bonnet.

"Bring him here," he shouted from under the open bonnet.

The blond cop lifted me up, shoved me to the engine compartment and carried on where he left off with the Indian cop by the guardrail. The warmth of the engine thawed whatever calm remained in me. The horses' hooves now stomped in unison. I knew the game was up when the older cop produced from his pocket a white cloth and a half-liter bottle of transparent liquid.

"You say this car is a rebuild?"

"Yes, sir, it is a rebuild," as my heart sank.

In the township, they say no altered engine has ever passed the liquid test. He soaked the cloth under vivid torchlight. The hooves amplified in my head. He rubbed the damp cloth over the engine number.

"Go on, take a look for yourself."

The torch was steady over the engine number.

"You say the car is a rebuild, mechanic? Explain to me why the original engine number of this car was ground off and new numbers stamped over it?"

The unravelling scene was clearer than day under the brightness of artificial light. The original numbers appeared clearly under the new numbers. He ran the original numbers on his radio.

"I said 'explain,' mechanic."

I faked incredulity to the best of my abilities. "You have no words now, mechanic."

"I don't know anything about the engine number. I bought the car smashed and I worked on it, sir."

He shook his head and leaned on the guardrail, the radio over his ear.

I looked around. No trees, only freshly cut grass. Even if I tried to get away there was absolutely no cover. I flirted with martyrdom for a moment, picturing my body broken under the passing cars. Suicide for the life I had chosen.

"Explain, mechanic, why you are driving a car that was hijacked in Ballito where the owner was shot in the head?"

"I don't know anything about the engine number, sir."

"Well, mechanic, you are under arrest for hijack, attempted murder and robbery," he said, slamming the hood.

"Mtshali, I have a clever one here; maybe he will talk to you."

He shouted to the anaconda 330i. To the driver who was not part of the attack formation.

"Bring him here," Mtshali replied.

The Indian cop escorted me to Mtshali. I sat in the back seat, my bones wobbly like shaking jelly. The cop's words rang in my head—attempted murder, hijack, robbery. Mtshali was on a call muted to my ears, for nothing else registered in my head but those words. I turned my head back to my glider, my first car.

The blond cop was eating my chips, which he had laid out on the roof of my car. By the guardrail the Indian cop was on his cellphone. Droopy-face was on a slow search of the cabin. Steady touches on the dashboard and its compartments. He disappeared from view and came up with the Mandrax pack from under my seat.

The three huddled over the pills laid out on the bonnet. They looked at me and shook their heads. The search turned brutal after that. The leather upholstery was cut in search of more drugs. It was only a matter of minutes before they opened the boot and cut the spare tire. Mtshali finished his call. With a step that suggested extreme boredom, he joined the three to look at the evidence on the bonnet.

The outcome of the meeting was this: the Indian cop drove my 328i; the white cops took all my pills into their Chevy Lumina and led the convoy; I rode with Mtshali in the anaconda 330i at the back.

The Lumina branched off at the Gateway off-ramp with a flicker of blue light.

Mtshali was a tiny man. Lean, with almost no body fat. Sparse wrinkles of middle age creased his face.

I caught his eyes in the rear-view mirror; he looked bored to the point of indifference.

"You are so arrested. Attempted murder, hijack, robbery, drug dealing. You'll be lucky if you don't get life for this."

"I don't know anything about the engine number, I swear."

"I am talking to you because I thought you were smart. It won't help you sticking to your story. It is a lie, and a stupid one at that. You might as well shut up; you deserve to go to jail for being so dumb."

I leaned back, away from his eyes, and searched my brain for a new approach.

"I can guess where you are from. We know Umlazi boys hustle cars. You are stupid. How can you be out in a car hijacked hardly a month ago? We are still looking for it. Stupidity should be number one on your charge sheet. You just could not wait to drive it—not even a few months. Which section do you come from in Umlazi?"

"M Section."

"How far away from Mama Mkhize's Tavern?"

"On the same street. I live in the house at the ring."

"I used to drink at Mama Mkhize's way back when I still lived in the township. I am talking about twenty years back, when it was still the original Mama Mkhize, not her daughter. How is M Section now? Last time I heard, people said it was a jungle over there."

"It's just the odd incident now. Mostly it is quiet."

"Just you and your cars and drugs."

I found his eyes again. With all the sincerity and honesty of a beggar, I laid out my new approach.

"Mr. Mtshal…"

"What do you say?"

"Sir, is there nothing I can do to make this go away?"

"I doubt it."

"Nothing at all, sir? Say I have something maybe you want?"

"The problem with you young boys is, I can listen to you now but the whole township will know what we talked about."

"It won't be like that, Mr. Mtshali, I swear."

"What is it we are talking about here, all these promises, for what? You are in trouble here. Problems as big as yours require even bigger solutions."

"I have cash in my room at home. How much can make this go away, Mr. Mtshali?"

My fate lay in the hands of this lean, bored man. He did not say a word for a while. A flicker of his lighter ignited a cigarette. His indifferent eyes out the window, he sank back into the bucket seat. I conditioned my mind to accept the possibility of years behind bars. My own eyes disappeared from the frame of the rear-view mirror. My gaze fell to my lap, and streams of tears soaked the fabric of my track pants.

After what seemed like forever, Mtshali let out a cough. He slowed down and flashed bright lights at the Indian cop in my glider. Both cars parked in the yellow lane. He went to the Indian cop. After a quick chat, they came over to me.

They looked at each other, unsure as to who was to start. Mtshali stared into the distance.

"Go on," Mtshali said.

"I was telling Mr. Mtshali that I have money in my room at home, sir. You can name the price."

"We are talking about cash in your room, not cash you are going to borrow from a friend or get from an ATM," the Indian cop stated matter-of-factly, his bushy eyebrows immobile.

"It is in my room, sir."

"Business must be good, mechanic. You think you can handle a four-man payoff?"

"I can do whatever is needed of me to make this disappear, sir."

They left me in the car. The odd car passed by and flashed lights at them. They talked by the guardrail over a cigarette.

Mtshali walked back to me with an unhurried step. The Indian cop puffed on in the darkness.

"This is how it will go down. Twenty-five grand will make this go away."

A sliver of hope dissolved the lump in my throat.

"In my room I have twenty grand for sure; the rest you will get by the end of the week, Mr. Mtshali."

He shook his head, went back to the Indian cop. A passing car's lights swept over them. My heart jump-started, for in the light of the passing car I saw both nod their heads in agreement. Mtshali opened the door.

"Just to be clear again, we are talking about money that is in your room. When we get to your house, you will go into your room, get it, and come out."

"It is as you say, sir. It won't even take a minute."

We left the Indian cop on the road with my glider. The dash to the township was a trip in silence. In my heart the beat was hope on adrenaline.

We passed an accident scene in the exit lane just before the township. A taxi and a bakkie. Mtshali pressed hard on the accelerator pedal; the whole scenario was like a blur as we passed it. I stretched my head to look back, but it was already out of view. The Chevy Lumina was back on our tail—the two white cops in front, the Indian in the back seat.

We parked by the blue wall. The Indian cop removed the number plates from both cars. Mtshali turned to me.

"Do you have a key or will you knock?"

"I have a spare key in the backyard."

"Now listen to me; you will be in and out. If we feel you are taking too long we will come for you, and believe me you don't want to see that. Will you be able to get it with handcuffs on?"

"I can, but it will not be as quick."

Mtshali opened my door and unlocked the handcuffs. Blood dripped from the gash on my wrist. I wrapped my T-shirt over it. The white giants secured the backyard; Mtshali and the Indian cop disappeared into the shadows of the front yard.

Under blocks in the backyard, in clear sight of the white cops, I found the spare key. All the people in my street were deep in sleep, with lights out. Even Mama Mkhize's was dark. I opened the kitchen door, tiptoeing to my room. I took all the money from under the mattress and piled it into a plastic bag—even the coins.

I locked the kitchen door and sprinted to the gap in the blue wall. Mtshali and the Indian were in the anaconda, the two white cops in their Lumina. The back door of the anaconda was ajar. I ran straight to it, got in with the plastic bag on my lap and closed the door. We drove off.

Anxiety overtook hope on adrenaline, for we left the township. My part of the deal was done, I thought; they would leave me somewhere in the township. But we kept going, the Lumina bringing up the rear. In minutes, the scene outside my window turned from township to rural. The last landmark I saw was the tiny town center of Umbumbulu. It was impossible to measure the distance we covered after that, for Mtshali drove fast.

We took a left in the dark onto a zigzag of gravel road. The Lumina was right on our tail, sometimes invisible under the clouds of dust we left behind at speeds too high for gravel roads.

We stopped in the middle of a road that sliced through a sugar cane plantation. They all got into the Lumina. The lights shining into the anaconda were so bright that I could see a strand of black hair on the headrest of one of the black leather seats.

They counted the money. I thought of Vusi, who had been found in a ditch. My eyes turned to the waving sugar cane. If they killed me here, who would find my body?

I shed tears for my life at the hands of four strangers. I cried for the angle from which I had embraced manhood. To always be happy and have things no matter what the cost. I cried for my mother, my father and for Nu. And for my girl Nana and her eyes. For them not knowing where I was buried. My head slumped. Who was I, to break that many hearts? I prayed that none of them would have to identify my body if I met a brutal death.

The search for consolation proved fruitless. My blurry eyes looked far ahead to the half-moon that shaded the night blue. Above the open sugar cane fields, the sky looked elevated, with stars in clusters.

Mtshali stepped out of the Lumina. It reversed and turned, the Indian and two white cops inside. They left us in a ball of dust.

"Get out," Mtshali said. I stepped out.

"Listen to me carefully. There is a police station five kilometers up the road. I have already called my guy there; he is coming to get you. When you get to the charge office you will say you hiked from Ixopo, but the man who gave you a lift robbed you and left you on this road. You did not see the number plates of the car. The blood on your wrist is from the fight you had with the man. Do you get what I am telling you?"

"Yes, Mr. Mtshali, I get it."

"You better get it, because if I hear that you said otherwise, I will bring you here, kill you and bury you in this sugar cane. I suggest you start walking."

"Thank you, Mr. Mtshali."

"Don't thank me yet. The cash you gave us is short by four grand. I want it next week or this whole deal is off."

"You will get it, sir."

"Tell anyone about this and I will bury you here."

He reversed, turned and left me in a cloud of dust. I stood still for a while until he disappeared.

I jogged in the direction he had told me to follow. It was like the sugar cane was whispering in the wind. The chilly breeze cooled me, for I opened my lungs. With each stride I ran faster. The rural night was plain creepy. The whispering sugar cane, a chilly breeze and singing insects ruled the air. I ran frantically when I saw the lights of a car coming down a treacherous hill. Waving like a madman, I flagged it down. It was a police van.

"Get in," said the cop driver.

We swung back uphill. I sat next to him, out of breath and words. He was quiet too, and hardly looked at me. He just shoved the van over gravel.

At the police station, I animated my story to the lady cop at the front desk.

Genuine concern filled her face.

"And you did not see the number plates?" she said.

"No, I did not see the number plates; the man was killing me."

"Since you described the car, we will be on the lookout for it. It is a pity you did not see the number plates. We have a van leaving for Durban in the morning. The officers can drop you off along the way."

My room for the night was a cell, my bed a thin piece of foam. The cell smelled of feces, urine and blood. I declined food. For the whole night I sat on the foam mattress. I felt the chilly breeze again and put on my bloodied T-shirt. The blankets bundled in a corner stank of urine. I sat in the center of the cell the whole night, my hand over my nose, but it was an inadequate filter against the stench. Not even the chilly winds that whistled through a high window could drive away the odor. At least the cracked frosted glass allowed for some sort of view—a portion of the bluish night sky and clusters of stars.

Glad, relieved and sad, I exhaled. I felt glad that I had found a way out of the mess, relieved that I was not going to prison, and sad for the money I had lost. I also realized how in debt I was. The ecstasy I owed no one as it was my own cash I had lost. I owed Mdala

YOUNG BLOOD

seven grand for the Mandrax pills. Plus, the four thousand I owed Mtshali. My money had gone from twenty-plus thousand to minus eleven grand in less than two hours.

In the morning, I rode in the back of the police van to the township. The door was bolted from the outside and the flaps on the sides of the canopy rolled down, so I sat in darkness. It was a beautiful cool morning, but I only got snippets of the freshness in the five steps or so from the cell to the van. Low clouds in neat balls dotted the indigo sky. A fresh, damp morning wind filled my lungs. Each cloud made its own shade on the green, rolling hills. Mtshali's plan was flawless. Even if I wanted to charge them with bribery—which I certainly did not—who would believe me if I did not know the way to the spot where the shakedown went down? Twenty-five grand was not too high a price to pay for my freedom, I consoled myself.

My body bounced and banged as the van rose and fell. I took every blow from the bumpy track. Twenty-five thousand rands for my freedom was a bargain. Convinced by this conclusion, it once again became my consolation.

After about an hour of gravel, we changed to the smoothness of tar. I closed my eyes and pictured home.

I opened my eyes when the van stopped and the canopy door was unbolted. Blinding light nullified the darkness. My eyes adjusted.

"Why are you not getting out? Is this not where you said we should drop you off?"

I stepped out of the van at 2524 Close. It was close to midday, the streets empty. The sun was out in earnest;

dry, hot winds dried my nostrils. The oppressive heat heavy on my bones, I trudged on home, body stiff like my father's at the end of the day. Ma was asleep. I took a bath, dressed the wound on my wrist, counted all my blessings and slept.

Legs, chest, back, face and head—my whole body was damp with sweat when I woke up. In the mirror in my room, I looked like I had just walked a mile in drizzle. A cool afternoon breeze blew the curtains. I opened my bedroom windows to their limit. My body immobile, the curtains pulled to the far ends of their rails, I surrendered to the afternoon breeze. Light gray clouds, dense as if from an erupting volcano, shrouded the sky.

I splashed water on my face in the bathroom. I heard my mother's laughter through the bathroom window. It came from somewhere in the backyard.

My father was under a Toyota van, his toolbox open by the front wheel. Ma was sitting on the bench, speaking in low tones with Dad, her laughter punctuating their hushed chatter.

"Here he is! For days I haven't seen you," Ma beamed at me.

"I've been here since midday. I was asleep, Ma. I was tired."

"What happened to your hand?"

I sat down next to her on the bench.

"It was cut by the fan behind the radiator."

"How bad is it?"

"Not that bad, Ma."

"Here, I have something for you."

She gave me a brochure from a technical college. Carpentry, welding, boiler-making, motor mechanics, panel-beating, secretarial courses—it was all there.

"It is not far, just outside the township. You don't need matric to do the courses. I want you to talk to the teachers there, find out what you like. Maybe next year you can study there."

"Okay, Ma. I will go tomorrow, but can we afford it?" I said.

"Don't worry about that, Sipho. My stokvel is paying out in January so you will have registration money. The fees will be payable; I am in line for promotion at work," Ma said.

"Take the R10 on the kitchen table. We are out of bread. Buy a newspaper with the change."

This came from under the Toyota van, where my father was in a struggle with the exhaust system.

The R10 note was under the kettle on the kitchen table. In my room, under the mattress, I looked for cash. I was thirsty and I craved a cigarette. Not a cent was there. I looked under my bed, raided all the pockets of my clothes. Nothing. On the stand next to my bed, sheltered by a tipped bottle of body lotion, I found a R1 coin. It was not enough for even one loose cigarette.

I bought bread and a newspaper at the shops. No change. At the back of the store, my friend Sticks held a freshly lit cigarette. I was guaranteed a puff because of the unspoken rule of township smokers— two smokers to one cigarette smoke means half the fag each.

"Did you read the paper?"

"I just bought it," I said.

Sticks shook his head. "So you haven't seen it?"

"What is in the paper, Sticks?"

"You did not see it?"

"See what?"

"The 325is you used to drive."

"What about it?"

"It is all there in the newspaper you are holding. The car was riddled with bullets. Your friend from Power, Musa, was in a gun battle in the city last night. He made the front page. There are pictures of the whole thing."

I leaned on the store wall. There was a photograph on the front page: from the number plate on the 325is, it was clearly Musa's ice-white glider. Bullet holes were clustered on the driver's door. Two foil-covered bodies lay in the parking bays. Two detectives crouched at the crime scene, squinting against the beach sand stirred up by the wind, their ties blown in opposite directions. In the background were breaking waves. Bloodied handprints smudged the driver's door of the 325is. Yellow police tape curved in the wind. The headline read, "SOUTH BEACH SHOOTING CLAIMS TWO."

I read the story on page two: Two men died in a shooting incident at the busy beachfront area last night. A third man who is allegedly the shooter is in critical condition under police guard in hospital. Police combed the scene till late morning today trying to piece together the chain of events. Police spokesman Siva Reddy said the critically wounded man is their main suspect. "Results from ballistic tests tell us that the two deceased died from gunshot wounds to the heads from the same gun, a .45 pistol. The same gun we found on the main suspect," said Supt. Siva Reddy. A morning jogger, Mr. Anthony Kleivers, alerted the police after he had stumbled across the gory scene: "I was on my morning jog when I saw the three bodies, guns and blood everywhere," he said. The police are asking for eyewitnesses to come forward with information.

I looked up from the newspaper and found that Sticks was no longer beside me. The sole reason he was at the back of the store was to chat up girls. He disappeared from view with a chick in school uniform.

My eyes were on the front page of the newspaper all the way home. Broken glass on the tarmac, the punctured back tires of the 325is, the bullet holes in the driver's door, the bodies covered with foil. I shook my head in disbelief and imagined the sheer violence of the scene. A girl with a familiar walk disappeared into the gap in the blue wall.

Nana was by the kitchen with Dad and Ma. I gave the paper to Ma on the bench and left the bread on the kitchen table. Nana followed me into the house.

She made up my bed before she sat down on it. Her face lacked the effervescence she had shown to my parents. No matter how hard I tried to find her eyes, they stayed hidden.

"Why are you not answering your phone?" she asked.

"I lost my phone yesterday after you said you couldn't talk. I think I left it at the garage where I filled up petrol. What was wrong with you yesterday?" I sat down on the bed.

"Nothing."

She came closer and laid her head on my lap. I looked for her eyes but she kept them away from me.

"What is wrong, baby?" Tears rolled down her

cheeks.

"I missed my period," she said.

"We'll go to a doctor and check what is going on. You can go to the doctor where you go for your checkups."

"No, I can't go to my doctor. What if my mother finds out?"

"You can go to another doctor, but give me a few days to get some cash together. How much do doctors cost now?"

"I wanted to go tomorrow. Don't worry about the money; I will take from my allowance. I just want you to be there, that is all."

"Of course I will be there."

I wiped her tears. We chilled on the bed for half an hour or so. We just sat, her head on my lap, my back to the wall. I tried to play the radio on her phone, but she moved it away. My hand caressed the curve at the back of her waist. Nana took my roaming hand in her hands. In the silence I made a photographic map of her face and stored it in a vault in my mind marked memories to never forget. I walked her to the taxi stop when her curfew neared.

Back home, Ma was over the stove; three pots steamed at once. Dad reversed the Toyota van to test it. Nu and most of the children in my street were running wild in the front yard. I sat on the backyard bench, the technical college brochure at my feet— blown there by the afternoon wind. I picked it up, but just looked at it. My head was still consumed by the picture on the front page of the newspaper. I imagined the sights and sounds of a gun battle in the city, the darkness like an amplifier to the blast of a .45. I stayed on the bench, my eyes gazing beyond the slopes of Power to a dusky horizon—thankful that I was not there.

"Sipho!" Nu shouted from the front yard. "What?"

"S-s-omeone here to s-s-ee you."

"Who is it?"

"I don't know."

A boy about my age was leaning on the front fender of a VW Golf IV GTI outside the blue wall. It was the first time I had seen him, but there was a familiarity to his face, like he was a younger version of someone I knew well.

"Are you Sipho?" he said.

"Yes."

"I have a message from my father, but it is for your ears only."

"For sure."

We sat in his car.

"My father said you must keep a low profile. He said do not call him or come to see him. Said you would understand that contact with Musa—or Sibani, for that matter—makes you a suspect. Keep your mouth shut. Don't move the pills until it all blows over. He said do not call him. Make sure you don't call him."

"Where is he?"

"He packed some clothes this morning and left. I don't think even my mother knows where he is. Where can I get cigarettes around here?"

"We can walk there. Maybe you can tell me the whole story."

He bought a packet of cigarettes at Mama Mkhize's. He looked exactly like Mdala. Younger, with a relaxed face, but his build and features were definitely Mdala's. He was dressed in understated lat-est-season Hugo Boss—linen shirt, jeans and loafers.

We lit cigarettes at Mama Mkhize's. When they were half smoked, we walked back to his car.

"My father was there with Musa. To do a number on the Cold Hearts. They did kill them; the whole thing made the front page. My father was shot in the shoul-der but managed to escape. He said Musa was shot real bad—one bullet in the neck, four ripped through the chest, three lodged in his leg. He said he only left Musa there because he thought he was dead."

"This is really fucked up."

"Yes, it is."

"You know, the pills Mdala is talking about I left at Musa's house yesterday."

"That is another thing he stressed. Do not go to Musa's house. The Serious and Violent Crimes Unit is handling the case, and they don't fuck around. Musa's house is under surveillance as we speak. If you have anything there, forget about it. If they catch you, they will make you talk. They have ways that turn the hard-est of crooks to rats."

"So I must keep a low profile."

"That is right."

"Where do you stay? I have never seen you when I visit your father."

"I study in Cape Town, so I live there most of the time."

"What are you studying there?"

"Chemical engineering."

"What year?"

"First."

"Can you leave me two cigarettes? I don't have a

cent on me. I left all the cash to my name at Musa's."

"Take the whole packet."

"Thanks."

"I am trying to quit, anyway."

"Tell me the secret when you do quit. What is your name?"

He opened the door and started his car. "Siboniso," he said and drove off.

That night in my room I detailed all my blessings in prayer.

❖

In the morning, I was ready before my father woke up. When he came out of the bathroom, he was his usual sprightly self. I ate a peanut-butter sandwich in the kitchen.

"You woke early today. Where are you off to?"

"I want to check out the technical college Ma was talking about."

"I don't think they open this early." Dad switched on the kettle.

"I want to take my time there, to see what I like."

He fished out R20 from the pocket of his overall. "Here is money for transport."

"Thanks, Dad."

The brochure was on the stand by my bed, next to another R20 Ma had given me. I picked it up and looked at the mirror for a second. I quickly turned away, for I did not like the look on my face: helpless, like I had lost my spark. Afraid. It was morning and the whole thing was real—Musa critical in hospital under police guard, Mdala in hiding. The worst part, the brewer of anxiety, was the total lack of communication. If Musa woke up and told the investigators everything, there would be no warning for me, no heads up, no phone call to tell me to run for it.

Dad stood in the backyard, his steaming enamel cup in his hand. I walked up my empty street to the taxi stop. I told myself, "If push comes to shove, what will be will be. I am not running away."

I was early at the technical college; the gates were still locked. The tiny stall next to the gate was open. A fresh-faced Rastafarian was setting out his display of sweets and cigarettes. He connected a payphone to a car battery and checked for the dial tone.

Students trickled through in small groups. Most made the stall their first stop for a morning cigarette. I followed suit and bought one. A security guard unlocked the gates. I released cigarette smoke from within a crowd of students—invisible. No one paid any mind to me, and I liked that. It was mostly boys, but there were a few girls I guessed to be taking secretarial courses. All around me was morning chatter. I heard bits about the weekend soccer game; someone went on about a wild weekend, complete with vivid animation about a car race. A joker killed a group of girls with laughter. Inside the college premises, the crowd dispersed into classes. I headed straight to the reception desk.

The secretary gave me directions to the office of the motor mechanics lecturer. I knocked and opened the door to a too cheerful "come in." A short, stocky white man laid out the motor mechanics course in a thick English accent.

"So if you attend all the classes and tutorials, you

will not have a problem," he said at the end of a well-rehearsed speech.

I left his office convinced, clutching a brochure specific to motor mechanics.

I called Nana at the payphone outside the college gates.

"We'll meet at The Wheel shopping mall. There is a doctor there. Wait for me by the seaside entrance. I'll be there in thirty minutes," she said.

I did not feel the thirty minutes. In the shade of the steps at the entrance of The Wheel, I watched the city-street bustle. Taxis offloaded passengers and picked up others. The ocean was visible through alleys lined with bars and flats. The sparkle of a summer sun headlined the horizon. It was the first day of the year that really felt like summer. Girls were out, convinced by the Durban summer sun that less was more. The steps of The Wheel were like a catwalk. I was right in the front row.

Nana stepped out from the bass throb of a taxi, fresh like the day we first met. Her face was so serious we did not even greet or kiss. Hand in hand, we went up the escalators to the doctor's office.

Four patients were ahead of us in the waiting area. Nana gave her details at the counter in the hushed tones we use at the doctor's.

There were only car magazines on the table in the waiting area. Most were current. I browsed through them. Nana stared at me, but when I looked at her, she turned sharply away. My cool demeanor came undone when her name was called.

My hands were clasped, but it was too late for

prayer. I wondered if such a thing was possible. Me, a father to be? What the hell was I going to tell my child? I dried my sweaty palms on my T-shirt.

It did not help that Nana came out with her head down. Her step fast, she motioned with her head that we were leaving.

"What did the doctor say?" I asked on the escalator. She did not answer until we were at the taxi stop.

"It was nothing. He says it happens sometimes. Said it is important that we use condoms," she smiled.

❖

It was the year of a stubborn winter that lasted well into spring. I was with my girlfriend at the beach the day summer convincingly won. We took a taxi to North Beach. On the short trip we clasped hands in our own world, a place where there was nothing but puffy white clouds of elation and green mountains of relief.

Before we got to the takeaway shops by the beachfront, Nana tugged at my hand.

"Here," she whispered and shoved a crumpled R100 note into my hand.

I bought two burger, chips and cold drink combos. We sat at an outside table, our eyes looking out to sea.

"So you went to the school?"

"Yes, baby."

"Find anything you like?"

"Yes, motor mechanics. I already know all there is to know about cars anyway."

"We'll have more time together, with me in tech and everything."

"For sure," I said.

Her eyes were back, and they pierced past mine like she saw what was cooking in my brain. It was my turn to look away. We chilled and munched down.

Taxi to taxi, we reached the township by early afternoon. When we got to her stop, I watched her until she was out of view.

❖

My father was under a Toyota Conquest in the backyard. I got into my overalls and joined him.

"What is wrong with this one?"

"Gearbox; it does not take gear three and five." He slid out and handed me a spanner.

"There is a nut I cannot reach."

I lifted the jack higher. Under the car, I looked for the unreachable nut.

"Did you go to the school?"

"Yes, Dad."

"Find anything you like?"

"Motor mechanics is the only course I can do there."

"Good. Because you have a bit of know-how, it will be an advantage. How is your friend Musa? I saw the mess he is in."

"He is in deep trouble, Dad. They say the wounds are serious."

"Too bad. The ancestors don't give warnings when they say 'no.'"

The nut was stiff. I turned the spanner gently lest I break it. My father disappeared into the kitchen.

The nut was off when he returned with his steaming enamel cup. He sat down on the bench and sipped from the cup. Instantly he rose, arms tight over his stomach.

"What is wrong, Dad?"

"I need the toilet. The chilies I ate yesterday are acting up." He left the enamel cup on a block.

I closed the kitchen door, sat on the bench and smoked a cigarette. My view was the slope of Power: a picture out of the blue, framed exactly like the canvas I had seen in my dream at Vusi's aftertears party. The shacks on a slope were the top part of the view. In the bottom left corner sat the rusted chassis of a car. The ear of a green enamel cup atop a block was at the bottom right corner. More blocks filled the rest of the base. Over the blocks, a burning cigarette sat snug between the fingers of what was undoubtedly my grease-covered hand.

Shaken, I looked over to 2524 Close. By Mama Mkhize's Tavern, Ma was struggling with groceries. I stubbed out the cigarette and ran to help her. I unpacked the groceries in the kitchen.

"Why did you not say it is so bad with your friend?"

"I just heard, Ma," I lied.

"I was in a taxi with his aunt; she says it is only a matter of time."

"Where is he?"

"King Edward Hospital."

"Do they allow visitors?"

"Only family, and she is the only family he has."

"Is it really that bad?"

"They say it is only a matter of time. His aunt said it is better he passes on, because the charges he'll be up against will keep him in jail for life. How did it go at the school?"

"I talked to a teacher there and I like it, Ma."

"Which course did you like?"

"Motor mechanics."

"So next year you can study there?"

"Yes, Ma, I will study."

❖

November turned into a buzzing December. The trees on my street were covered in lush green leaves. Under cars with my father I made some cash—not crazy hustler money but survival cash for smokes and the occasional day out with Nana. Musa was still in hospital, the prognosis grimmer with each month.

It was a Sunday, our day off. There was absolutely nothing to do, so I just sat on the blue wall. Ma and Nu were in church, Dad at the funeral of a distant relative.

A red dolphin-shaped BMW 328i pulled over at Mama Mkhize's Tavern. It was exactly like mine, but with tinted windows. A tiny, bored-looking man disappeared into Mama Mkhize's. A bottle of Jameson was in his hand when he came out. His was a face I remembered instantly. Mtshali.

He turned at the ring and stopped by the blue wall. The driver's window rolled down. He killed the volume on the stereo. His index finger was over pursed lips.

"Shh, never say a word," he said and drove off.

His dry, forced laugh lingered with me long after he disappeared. Mtshali never pitched up for his R4 000. Months passed; we embraced a new year.

From my first class at the technical college, I realized that my mind no longer drifted into a maze of tangents. I concentrated for the forty minutes the classes lasted. They teach about engines and issues of interest to me, I told myself.

One afternoon at the end of my first week in school—the February sun so relentless that I finished my classes, went home and slept—I heard the news under the shade of trees by the blue wall. Sticks crept next to me.

"Did you hear?"

"Hear what, Sticks?"

"Your friend from Power—Musa?"

"What about him?"

"He passed away this morning in hospital."

My heartbeat was normal; I looked away from Sticks for fear of tears, but my eyes were dry. I looked at the ground and pulled out a cigarette.

"Did you hear what I just told you?"

"I heard you, Sticks. Musa passed away this morning," as I dragged light puffs.

The sky was dark blue with clouds of fluffy white. I said a silent goodbye to my friend Musa. I knew I would not go to his funeral. Undercover cops would be there, waiting to connect the dots. I passed the cigarette to Sticks.

My mind never again drifted in class. They teach about things of interest to me, I told myself. But, in retrospect, I know that I concentrated in class because of everything I saw in the year that I turned seventeen.

YOUNG BLOOD

ACKNOWLEDGEMENTS

Thank you, Ma and Babo,
for raising me in a happy home.
And my people—
Meme, Thobeka,
EE, Loi and Mbali—
for laughter always.

SIFISO MZOBE was born in Umlazi, Durban, where he also went to school. After attending St. Francis College, he studied journalism at Damelin Business Campus in Durban. He currently works for a community newspaper as a journalist.

9 781946 395481